Winner of the Jan Michalski Prize for Literature

Longlisted for the Man Asian Literary Award

Shortlisted for the Haus der Kulturin's
International Literary Award

"Examine[s] the complexities and moral ambiguities of the experience of the poor and forgotten, mixing the brutality of that world with the lyricism of the Persian language."

—*THE NEW YORK TIMES*

"Dowlatabadi combines the poetic tradition of his culture with the direct and unembellished everyday speech of the villages. With this highly topical new novel Mahmoud Dowlatabadi, Iran's most important novelist, sheds light on the upheavals, which haunts his country until today."

—MAN ASIAN LITERARY PRIZE
NOMINATION CITATION

"A demanding and richly composed book by a novelist who stands apart." —*KIRKUS*

"You feel as though you're watching a horror movie set in Iran ... the foolish, sometimes heroic, and always pathetic victims and survivors of the Ayatollah's ghoulish revolution."

—ALAN CHEUSE, NPR

"Dowlatabadi draws a detailed, realist picture of Iranian life, especially that of the rural poor, in language that is complex and lyrical, rather than simplistic." —*THE FINANCIAL TIMES*

"*The Colonel* is a remarkable and important book ... A masterpiece." —*THE GLOBE AND MAIL*

"A pleasure to read ... Dowlatabadi is heralded as one of, if not the, greatest Iranian novelists, and *The Colonel* bears that out. That Dowlatabadi persists, despite having been at various times imprisoned, tortured and censored, is a testament to the Iran that could be, and that still can be." —*THE RUMPUS*

"It's about time everyone even remotely interested in Iran read this novel." —*THE INDEPENDENT*

"An affecting and beautiful novel." —*THE LITERARY REVIEW*

"Instructive ... A stirring tale replete with the hideous viscera of violent confrontation." —*BOOKLIST*

"An outstanding master achievement." —*DER SPIEGEL*

"This novel has what it takes to become a strong and irresistible window into Iran." —*DIE ZEIT*

"A very powerful work."

"Because of its honesty and indeed brutal clarity of language the novel has so far not been published in its original language, Persian ... [an] honest and truly literary account."

## PRAISE FOR *MISSING SOLUCH*

"Beautifully and incisively rendered, and imbued throughout with hope."

"There are some brilliantly tough pieces of writing ... [The original's] vigour comes through in translation."

"Brings *East of Eden* to mind ... Dowlatabadi knows a world that has seldom overlapped with the modern novel."

"Dowlatabadi has created a masterpiece."

MAHMOUD DOWLATABADI is one of the Middle East's most important writers. Born in 1940 in a remote farming region of Iran, the son of a shoemaker, he spent his early life and teens as an agricultural day laborer until he made his way to Tehran, where he started acting in the theater and began writing plays, stories, and novels.

Dowlatabadi pioneered the use of the everyday language of the Iranian people as suitable for high literary art. His books include *Missing Soluch*, published by Melville House and his first work to be translated into English, and a ten-book portrait of Iranian village life, *Kelidar*. In 1974, Dowlatabadi was arrested by the Savak, the shah's secret police force. When he asked what crime he'd committed, he was told, "None, but everyone we arrest seems to have copies of your novels, so that makes you provocative to revolutionaries." He was in prison for two years.

His novel *The Colonel* was shortlisted for the Haus der Kulturen der Welt Berlin International Literature Award, long-listed for the Man Asian Literary Prize, and the winner of the 2013 Jan Michalski Prize for Literature.

# THIRST

## MAHMOUD DOWLATABADI

TRANSLATED BY
MARTIN E. WEIR

MELVILLE HOUSE
BROOKLYN · LONDON

THIRST

First Melville House Printing: June 2014

Melville House Publishing          8 Blackstock Mews
   145 Plymouth Street   and   Islington
   Brooklyn, NY 11201          London N4 2BT

mhpbooks.com    facebook.com/mhpbooks    @melvillehouse

ISBN: 978-1-61219-300-7

Library of Congress Control Number: 2014944157

Manufactured in the United States of America
1 3 5 7 9 10 8 6 4 2

# 1

SOMEWHERE, ON SOME SPOT here on planet Earth, a shell is discharged from the muzzle of a gun. No, let me rephrase that … Somewhere, on some spot on planet Earth, a leaden shell, heavy and destructive, is fired from the long, wide barrel of a heavy mortar. We can't be more precise than that, unless we know how much explosive material is contained in that almost cone-shaped shell. But we don't, and perhaps the person who orders the firing button to be pressed doesn't know either. But why am I imagining a finger pressing a button at all? Maybe it's a switch that is flicked instead. Up or down? How should I know? What difference does it make, and why should the components of a killing machine be important when they make such a fearsome unified whole? So, let's just say a shell was fired in order to drop from the sky somewhere on this Earth – after following a trajectory that in my mind's eye, seems long – to explode, destroy and ignite a whole area and send a cloud of smoke billowing into the air.

Without doubt, whenever a shell is fired, it must have an intended target. If possible a specific one and if not a non-specific one. But on the particular scrap of land where our tale will unfold, the target happens to be both specific and non-specific. Specific because the setting is a battle-ground, and non-specific because someone far away, out of sight, has surmised that this area is a centre for resistance in the form of guerrilla warfare. And so, on the basis of this assumption, a bombardment began at sundown, starting at an inconspicuous location and eventually surrounding the young men of this story; and since it is nighttime and therefore impossible to show any flame or light, it is not clear how many from that small group survived. An order to retreat has been given, but no-one can tell whether anyone has escaped from the circle of fire in time, or whether they are lying on the ground at a distance, half-alive. Likewise, it's unclear whether anyone has remained in position, dead, alive or wounded. Even if anyone should utter a sound, the din caused by the hail of bullets doesn't allow the soldiers to hear each other's voices. The person who is moaning and calling for water must be quite close, in any event. But close to whom? Perhaps to those who are still alive and well.

Any number of shells have rained down. But that water tank still remains standing in one of the valleys between the hills up ahead. In all likelihood, it has shuddered several times from near misses, causing the water inside to spill over and run down the outside of the tank, but it's still standing in the same gulley, seemingly immune to all gunfire. The tank should be safe for the time being, as it's not in the enemy's direct line of sight; unless, that is, their troops crawl out of their trenches, charge down the hill and happen upon it. But it seems that they have not yet been given the order to do so; if they did advance down the hill, they might find themselves trapped in the same gulley as the water tank, in plain sight and within range. Which would mean that anyone who opened fire could kill as many of them as he had bullets. So the hope is that, at least until this intense bombardment is over, the water tank will remain unscathed, while those soldiers who have fallen on the path leading from the tank to the trenches will also stay where they are, dead or alive. In the distance, between the brow of the hill and the water tank, some enemy soldiers have fallen dead or dropped to the ground: some of them before reaching the tank and some on their way back with full water bottles, some of which may still be intact, dangling from their necks and shoulders. But we can also assume that many of those flasks will be mangled and riddled with bullet holes. Now anyone who tries to fetch water will first have the difficult task of finding and quickly gathering up any empty, intact flasks before dashing down to the tank to get water.

But what if all the flasks are full of holes?

'*Al-atash, atash … atashaan.*'*

It's the captive enemy who has piped up. 'Shut him up!' one of the men responds. 'Perhaps,' he continues, 'the hail of fire might cease if the enemy realises that we've taken one of their number prisoner.' Another says with a bitter smirk: 'Yeah, right, like they're capable of showing pity!'

'What are we to do then?'

'Good question, what are we to do! It's not like it's our decision to make.'

'How many of us are left?'

'Only you, as far as I know. Until the sun rises a bit higher we can't tally up the survivors.'

---

* Arabic, meaning 'Thirst, thirst… I'm thirsty.'

'We mustn't raise our voices.'

'*Atash ... atash ... atash! Ah ... ah ... jor'a ...*'*

'He's getting restless. And my wrist feels like it's about to snap; he keeps tugging on the rope. I think he must be dehydrated; what should we do with him?'

'Whatever's best for us. If you know his language, tell him there'll be no water until the shooting stops. How many men should we martyr for some water? He saw what happened with his own eyes! Tend to his wound again. If the bleeding stops, he'll survive.'

'Let's radio for help again. The radio telephone is still working.'

'When the order to retreat arrives, then we'll retreat. But right now, in this situation ... we can't.'

'So what do we do? What should we do?'

'Exactly what we're doing now. Just keep your voice down. Now tell me what else is on your mind.'

'I'm just thirsty, so thirsty.'

'Me too ... who isn't, if they're still alive?'

'After sending in those RPG rounds they must reckon there's no one left.'

'Let's hope to God that they make that mistake. That's why we must remain silent. Stop that young man's mouth with a rag. Thirst is driving him mad and might make him scream all of a sudden. Do it now, gag him, will you?'

'His injuries are fatal, though. Why don't we at least untie his wrist from mine?'

'It's a leg wound. His hands are fine.'

---

* Arabic, meaning 'Thirst ... thirst ... thirst! Ah ... ah ... a gulp ...'

'That's what I'm saying. He can't escape!'

'Maybe not escape, but he could stick a bayonet in one of our backs when we're not looking. It's his duty as a soldier – and he's crazy now, as well.'

'So let me tie his hands together.'

'What if he unties them? Then you'll be the first to get a bayonet in the back; he's your prisoner.'

'What can I do then? I'm his captive too, as it stands; why don't I just put him out of his misery?'

'No need. His comrades might well see to that.'

'How long do you think we'll survive?'

'Till we shrivel up and die from lack of water.'

'When will it end?'

'What?'

'The night!'

'I'm worried about the other trenches. Stay where you are, don't move! The other trenches aren't stirring either; I don't know if they're alive or dead. When the day finally dawns properly, we'll know for sure, as long as …'

'As long as they don't just start bombing us again?'

'Would you like me to write them a pleading letter?'

'You think now is a good time to joke …?'

'What then? You want me to reprimand you instead?'

'No! I've got an idea … Let's exchange the captive for water!'

'Huh?'

'Our prisoner … for water. How about it?'

'How do you know what's going on over there? Maybe they've taken one of our men prisoner too.'

Yes, maybe. Looking across to that hill, the far hill,

the foot of the hill, the meadow, with metal shrapnel, spent shells, armoured personnel carriers, fire and suffocating smoke that keeps billowing up, ever higher into the sky ... and then more meadows and mountain passes and ditches and trenches and troop units, personnel carriers, comings and goings, trampled ditches – all half-burnt. Earth, earth, water, water, water beyond the Shatt al-Arab, streams flowing on this side and the far side of the Shatt, a quiet city, houses in darkness and people breathing. People who are alive. But not necessarily. We cannot know what sort of lamp the other author behind the black curtains is using as the source of the weak light that illuminates his small kitchen table. A lantern or a hurricane lamp; a kerosene lamp or a candle? A candle for sure, a dim light; just enough to illuminate a white sheet of paper, which absorbs the light from the candle, stuck on a terracotta plate. The candle flame is flickering a bit, like in days of old, making the author appear like those ancient scribes who copied even older manuscripts: manuscripts in Kufic script, rewritten in Naskh.* They developed hunched backs, those scribes, with their necks and shoulders constantly bent over, while the light of their eyes grew dim from early on, setting them on the inevitable path to blindness; and even if they didn't go completely blind, their sight would gradually diminish. They spent their time copying books for the libraries of some caliph or emir or other, which in all probability were seldom read – such a difficult and strenuous

---

*Kufic and Naskh are two calligraphic forms of Arabic script. Kufic is older and more geometric, while Naskh is cursive.

task, one wonders what prompted them to take it up in the first place! Sitting crouched on a small carpet, with one knee laid flat on the ground and the other bent in front of them, their notebooks balanced on the upright knee and the reed quill held in their right hand, one pot of black ink and one pot of purple, with quills and quill cases next to the inkpots on a wooden tray or a plank – scribbling away incessantly until their lives came to an end!

At this moment, that other author, who has been cast unexpectedly back into the past, is sitting not on a carpet or beside a wooden tray containing his writing materials, but instead, at a kitchen table, on a bamboo chair. Sweat, brought on by the intense heat, has soaked his head and neck, his chest and his armpits too, and the electric fan on the ceiling isn't working because the city's power is out. Now and then, he wipes the sweat off his brow and from round his neck with a handkerchief he has placed on the table, and then pauses for a moment, resting his forehead on the pad of the handkerchief clasped in his left hand and closing his eyes, while a comfortable Lamy fountain-pen lolls between the fingers of his right hand. He has marked the end of the last paragraph he wrote with a full stop and is about to move on to the beginning of the next line. He half-opens his eyes and glances at his sleeping family. His mother, his wife and their children. There they all are, sleeping peacefully – lucky for them, he thinks, that they are sleeping so soundly, blissfully unaware that in retribution for the missiles and bombs that have been unleashed upon the other side's cities, a bomb or missile might drop at any moment from the sky and fall directly on the roof of their house, burying them in a hole in the ground. No, on reflection, he decides nothing of that sort is going to happen and stretches out his hand to pull a single cigarette from the packet, puts it between his lips and reaches for the matchbox when he suddenly recalls that, in amongst all the reports of his country's battles and battlefield gains, he may have seen an item somewhere – was it in the newspapers, on the radio or on television? – about the risks of passive smoking. And so he keeps the unlit cigarette between his lips for a few moments, rolls it around his mouth and thinks of smoke, fire – the smoke behind the hill and the front-line trench, or the trenches in which the characters of his story are lying hidden, behind a protecting barrier of sandbags. He sees the commander of the reconnaissance regiment suddenly stubbing out his half-smoked cigarette on the trench wall and cursing everything that goes by the name of 'air force' in armies all around the world. 'Get down!' he yells, flinging himself into a hand-dug ditch; crouching there, all he can hear is explosions, screams and then more explosions near the base of the hill. He can feel the ground shaking, and the dirt crumbling from the walls of the trench onto his back and shoulders. The air-strike is heavy and the corporal is certain that after such an assault, his line of communication with his HQ behind the lines will have been cut. Twenty-four hours at least will be needed to remove all the corpses, and to regroup and plan a counterattack. So, on a sudden impulse, the other author at the kitchen table lights up his cigarette and writes: 'Under no circumstances should prisoners be killed! They are your captives, and are completely in your charge.'

'But you killed him! Why can't you keep your nerves under control?'

'Look behind you! Their charred bodies are still lying there. A whole company of our men has just been wiped out. Either incinerated or simply evaporated into thin air! Can't you see?'

'I'm not blind, of course I can see what's happened.'

'Jumped for joy and whooped, he did, when they bombed us; you didn't hear him, but *I* heard him alright; I was standing right next to him!'

'What about the other one? Him!'

'He's still alive. But he's fatally wounded. And no, he won't be able to stick a bayonet in my back, 'cos I've tied both his hands. He's lying somewhere over there. Where are we going to get water from now?'

'There's water down there. In that same water tank I've been defending against their attacks all day. I shot their last water-carrier – riddled his flasks with bullets and blew them up. And if any more of them try to fetch water, then I'll send them to join their dead brothers. Anyone making for the tank is plumb in my line of sight. Of course, they might all go mad from thirst and try and rush the tank. If they do that, I'll open up on them with the machine gun. But as for now, heave the one you killed out of the trench and roll him down the hill. If we keep him in the trench with us till tomorrow, he'll start rotting in the heat of the sun. Give him a good shove, we may have to stay here for some time yet.'

'What?'

'What other choice have we got? We've got to stay here

until help arrives; at least until we can get some bread and water.'

'Ah … water; bread and water. Yeah, if they hadn't hit our own water bowser I'd sneak over there under cover of darkness and bring us back some water and food. But … but what now? Are we just gong to sit here and wait for their pincer attack?'

'Don't tempt fate! They don't have the energy. Our forces gave them a real pounding up there a while ago. I don't see them standing tall, either. They're in the same boat as us.'

'But yesterday …'

'You mean earlier today, don't you? Or what's the time – I've lost track …'

'One in the morning. I do mean yesterday after all.'

'Alright. Calm down and let's see what we can do. What about the other trenches? Any sounds, any voices?'

'Not a peep. Silent as the grave.'

'Go and find us some water, even a single water bottle will do … Look at the stars!'

That was what he wrote, the other author, before glancing up at the clock in the wall niche. He couldn't make out what it said, so he removed the spectacles he wore to correct his short-sightedness from the bridge of his nose. Now he could make it out; the clock's hour hand was approaching one in the morning. But as he sat watching it, the second hand jumped! It skipped a second, and then another … and suddenly it seemed to be whizzing round ever faster by the moment. He wondered if this was even possible? Can time speed up at ground level? It wasn't like flying in a plane from one continent to the other; or like the velocity of a missile being fired from its launcher. This was pure time: time in the sense of time passing heavily and ponderously beneath the humid heat of the ceiling above his head as he smoked his cigarette, blithely ignoring the television's daily warnings about the dangers of smoking. No, what he was driving at was the true sense of time in its monotonous and fateful onward march. Or maybe he meant time in the sense of the corrosive dread that afflicted him, me and all of us; he imagined his children, right then immersed in their deep, innocent sleep, suddenly growing old and circling his coffin, placing his notebook and Lamy fountain pen beside his casket and intoning laments for him. Yes, that was what he was really talking about: time as a surgical procedure! Slicing away and discarding a horrific future from life, like an appendicitis operation. What a brilliant thought! He put his spectacles back on the end of his nose and stared at his final sentence. 'Look at the stars!'

Stubbing out his cigarette, he picked up the colourful handkerchief once more and wiped the sweat from his brow, before mopping his neck, armpits and the grey hair on his chest. A bowl of water was what he wanted now; it might have been mentioned on television that water was good for your health. He stood up and went over to fetch a bowl of water, into which he'd melted an ice cube, then returned to sit at the kitchen table again. He pondered on how to proceed with his story: beyond the battle zone of Hill Zero everything was now destroyed, and his characters' line of communication was broken; but now that they'd killed off one healthy captive and kept alive another who could speak a little Arabic, what would they do without water and food, given that no order had yet been received to fall back?

# 2

'WHEN WILL THIS NIGHT ever end?'

'Are you whingeing again! Just look at the stars, why don't you? For a moment I thought it was our young prisoner saying something ...'

'He can't, though. He can only toss and turn. What should I do with him?'

'Did you gag him with the handkerchief? Take it out now, or he'll choke! I told you to tie it over his mouth, not shove it down his throat! Get it out!'

'But I've only got one hand free ... how can I tie a knot with just one hand?'

'Don't you have teeth? Have the mice eaten them all, or what?* Use your teeth and your hand. I can't take my eyes off the front. Suppose they've gone crazy after that heavy bombing? Maybe they'll tuck their tails between their legs and clear off before the morning. The area behind them is a wasteland, it was blitzed.'

'Water, water ... all this prisoner of ours says when he opens his mouth is "*al-atash*". Come tomorrow we'll all roast in the sun from thirst.'

'There's still a long time to go till tomorrow ... what time is it?'

'One in the morning.'

---

* An idiom in Farsi.

'Good morning to you, then!'

'And to you … let me untie my hand, sir, and go and check on the others in the other trenches.'

'Wait until it's light. As you can hear, nobody's making a sound. Keep your ears to the ground.'

'You're right. I can't hear a thing.'

'Can you count how many of us are left?'

'You're not joking, are you? We were seven to start with, but now … we're just one and a half!'

'What's the deal with the half-a-person?'

'That's me! I'm half-a-person, aren't I, when one of my hands is bound … What are you thinking of? Please find a solution, or let me tie his hands and feet and throw him in a corner, or simply put him out of his misery … it'd only take one bullet. It's not like they haven't killed enough of our troops.'

'No! No! No! I've been told not to kill prisoners. Ordered by someone who'd give up his life for each and every one of us. Maybe what he told me was a sentence from the will he never wrote. He never wrote anything, ever. Not even a letter to his wife. He said this to me before his first and last leave of absence. My only hope, now that I'm teetering on a knife edge between death and life, and the only thing that's keeping me alive, is this short sentence that I heard during the brief time I was able to be at his side. A fleeting moment on a night like this very night. He had come to inspect us. I'd been told that was something he always did, without fail. He came quickly, he stayed briefly, and moved swiftly from trench to trench, inspecting everyone and everything, and I'm certain he didn't sleep more than three hours in an entire day. Who was he and what was he? I only wish I could see him one more time and ask him "Who *are* you?" But it didn't come to pass. I never had the chance again. Anyway, I suspect he wouldn't respond to such a question. I could see he wasn't one for talking much. His whole being was action. He expressed himself through deeds rather than words. Are you listening to me? He was a man of action, pure and simple. Prisoners must not be killed, he said! I'll leave you to make of that what you will. I know what I understand by it. This is a war, I'm well aware of that. They don't go round handing out cookies in war. They kill us and we kill them, sure. At least one enemy battalion was wiped out in our last counterattack and we chalked it up as revenge for their previous attacks. But a prisoner of war … you know, I thought a lot about that sentence. It's partly because a captive is a defenceless and submissive creature, but as far as I'm concerned that's just scratching the surface. Beneath it all there is another issue, that is, when a person is captured everything that makes up the way he appears to the world suddenly falls apart. His military honours, his uniform, his weapon and everything that he was carrying in his pockets or knapsack is taken away from him and suddenly you're looking at an ordinary man who's just the same as you, just like you were before you were called up. How can you fight a person who reminds you of yourself? What sort of argument can you have with him? He isn't even armed! He's not a soldier anymore …'

'What am I supposed to do with him then? Untie my hand, will you! At least grant me the same rights as you do to an enemy prisoner!'

'Okay, then, have it your way. Tie his hands together. But be careful, an enemy is an enemy no matter what.'

'What about his mouth?'

'Gag it so he can't scream, and put him in that corner where we can see him!'

'What did you say that commander's name was?'

'I didn't mention his name, did I?'

'No, actually, I don't think you did.'

'He wouldn't want his name to be repeated. He was a flame that was extinguished. He wanted to become like the ones who've already passed on.'

'Are you being poetic?'

'It's the absolute truth, I swear.'

'So, did you ever stop to think how a man like that could order an assault when he was sure hundreds would be killed?'

'No, I didn't. But I'm sure he believed in our right to defend ourselves.'

'It looks like this night will never end. Do you think we're under siege?'

'How long have you been in the army now?'

'Six months and seven days.'

'Let me give you a piece of advice. Maybe even a final parting word!'

'What?'

'Don't count the days. Even if you think you're in mortal danger, don't count them. And don't count them now. The night can't last forever. It's in its nature to be replaced by day. It can't stay in one place. It must pass. But if you tie yourself up in knots counting the passage of moments, you'll only make their passing slower and heavier. Just let night move at its own pace.'

'I'm thirsty ... and hungry.'

'Saying that over and over again won't fill your stomach or quench your thirst, either. Patience is the name of the game, patience! Let's be patient together. I'm your superior, so I could simply order you to be quiet, but I won't do that. Let's talk like friends or brothers instead, because this might be the last night of our lives. Let's stay calm.'

'Last night? The last night of ... if a person knows he's going to live for only one more night, what should he do?'

'That all depends on where he is.'

'I'm talking about here, where we are right now!'

'Here ... his most important task would be to grow four eyes, and to keep two glued to the front, fixed on that hill, and two at the back so we can't be taken by surprise from the rear.'

'But you ... you do something else as well as all that – you think! I bet you've been to university ...'

'It would be easy for you to think too, you don't need a university education. After all, all human beings think, but not all of them have been to university. Each person thinks to the extent of his knowledge.'

'But I ... when I think, I get to bad places; like how did I end up in this shitty situation? I keep turning that thought over in my mind.'

'Then stop turning it over, break the vicious circle! It won't solve the problem.'

'How can I do that?'

'It's quite simple. Imagine you're not alone. During the

first half of the night at least three or four individuals like you and me were slain in front of our eyes while trying to fetch some water to save us from dying of thirst. But it's still night, so how can we be sure? Maybe they aren't dead yet? What if they're lying down there, thirsty and wounded? Can you imagine how they're suffering right now? But if you apply your mind to it, you can break out of that vicious circle of thought, because it won't make any difference to the situation. Like it or not, here is where we are. And you can put any thoughts of deserting out of your mind too, because I have permission to shoot you in the back if you do. Even if I only shoot you below the knee you'll be crippled for life. If I'm feeling merciful, I'll fire into the ground behind you, and you'll succeed in your escape attempt and run directly into the enemy lines. In which case you'll end up being shot in the chest; you can be certain they won't bother with any "below the knee" nice-ties. But even if we assume none of these things happen and by chance you manage to survive, that's when the real problems begin for you: the desert, the sun, the thirst and the loneliness. Haven't you ever heard of how people who are lost in a desert are brought to their knees by thirst and fatigue? Then it will be the turn of pitiless vultures who will start by digging your eyes out of their sockets!'

'How do you know all this stuff? Did you read it in books?'

'Look, just don't think about it too much. You'll start imagining things. We'll be rescued tomorrow. We'll look at the weather, the light, weigh up the situation, and then act. So we'll be free. Free to rescue ourselves in any way we can.

Keep your spirits up! I told you the story of that lioness, didn't I? She'll find us tomorrow, I promise. We're not supposed to stay hunkered down on this hillside forever. Our next task is to find a way of breaking out of their pincer movement. Let me see what the opposite hill is up to. There's firing going on behind them as well. What we're engaged in now is a war of patience. Let's see which side will yield to impatience first, us or them? So think about good things!'

# 3

ON THE OTHER SIDE of the Shatt al-Arab, two tropical flies keep skimming over the heads of the author's wife and children. Their buzzing is constantly audible to the man, and he finds himself distracted by them in a most irritating manner; he becomes transfixed by the flies' restless gyrations and falls to wondering whether they might be a male and female engaged in a courtship ritual. They land on the little girl's purple cheek, grapple with each other and flit off again. The next place they alight is on his wife's toes, which are peeking out from under the sheet. He decides to get up and kill the flies ... but at the same time he permits himself a wry smile, as if to say, look, I can't even manage to find an effective way of shooing away a couple of flies. Worse still, I've wasted precious moments watching them, and neglected the fact that my publisher is waiting for what I am writing, and what I'm obliged to write is a piece that recalls the Battle of Qadisiyyah.* The flies and I, the night and the candle, the Lamy fountain pen and Saad Waqqas; bombers and floodlights; a machine gun that in a blink

---

* During the Iran–Iraq War (1980–88), Saddam Hussein's Iraq was fond of referring to the conflict as the 'second Qadissiyah', a reference to a battle in AD 636, when an Arab army under the Caliph Umar and Saad Ibn Abi Waqqas, a companion of the Prophet Muhammad, defeated the forces of the Persian Sassanid Empire. This decisive engagement led to the Arab conquest of Persia.

of an eye can raze an enemy column to the ground the instant it comes into view; bulldozers, tanks and armoured cars; military aircraft in supersonic flight, buttons … red and green buttons … alarms; the blood-drenched sword of Saad. How many times should I mention the fact that he ordered a palace to be built in whose entrance the gates of the seven cities of Kasra could fit? Or note that the gates and the palace were burnt down by order of the caliph at the time because, as the caliph said to Saad, you are following the ways of Persian kings, so I command you to live in a house made of reeds like the common people or soldiers! My Lamy fountain pen writes fluently, but it cannot locate Saad. Instead it is trapped amid the fire and smoke on Hill Zero, and again writes: 'Prisoners must not be killed!' But at the same time it is clear that this universal humanitarian principle will not be deemed acceptable and that, instead, the author will be expected to write: 'We do not kill captives – it is our enemies who show no mercy, even to prisoners; mercy they show not!'

They took him and showed him the prisoner-of-war camp. During this visit, as it turned out, the author – the owner of the fountain pen, which was a gift – witnessed a strange and incredible sight. The PoWs were badly shaven, with unkempt and bloody faces and eyes bloodshot from suffering. There were twenty-six alive, and one corpse: two convicts, with their hands tied back-to-back, were being paraded in front of a row of their fellow inmates because during the night they had smothered their cellmate to death. One of them had sat on the victim's legs and gripped his ankles tight while the other held a folded blanket over his mouth and sat on top of it until he suffocated. There they stood, two young men shackled together, beards just sprouting on their smooth, unscarred faces. They had not been forced to dry-shave their light stubble. On reflection, 'dry-shaving' isn't quite the right term; at nightfall, together with the pair of barber's razors that were allotted to the prison wing, two empty buckets were provided. These were to be used as chamber pots, and the urine was then used to wet the soldiers' faces for shaving. There was no escaping this unpleasant ordeal; a directive was issued to the effect that 'any beard that has not been properly shaved or is only partly shaved will be dry-shaved by your own hands in the morning, after which you'll be placed in solitary confinement!'

Afterwards the author was invited to the prison camp's office for a cup of Yemenite coffee and treated to a lecture about the atrocities committed by the enemy, hot from the front. He was also promised a full account of what had happened in the prison the previous night, as well as other incidents that 'are bound to be of interest to you ... do you take sugar?'

'Yes, just a little, thanks.'

'When we've finished our coffee, I'll take you to the other detention centres to give you a good idea of our magian enemy's wickedness! We keep young men under the age of eighteen and older civilians in separate quarters to prevent such crimes from recurring. But even so ...'

The author interrupted to say how he had read in history books that the Sassanids had once used to refer to their enemies as magi, or 'sorcerers'; those people who were conquered in Iran, and by our swords, converted to Islam. I'm amazed to hear that you still call them magi!

'You are naïve, my dear Katib.* The magi never converted. That's the official version, certainly, so that's the line we're obliged to take. But if they are not magi, then what are they? There's no insult too bad for the enemy, wouldn't you agree? Let's walk over there and I'll show them to you, and describe what they have done, case by case. I'll also present you with credible reports of atrocities like the mass murder of prisoners.'

The nonplussed author made a mental note to go back to his history books and dictionaries and look up the exact etymology of such words, and as he walked out into the desert beside the prison camp's officer, he focused his attention on two points: first, the meanings of words, and second, Hill Zero and what fate befell the characters in his story. He always obeyed the writer's rule of thumb that you should read through the final passage of what you had written the previous night to get yourself properly steeped in the atmosphere of your tale, and when you got up from your desk at the end of the day, you should leave something hanging so you could pick up the thread the next day. Lost in his own thoughts, despite himself, all he could remember from last night's writing was this phrase 'prisoners must not be killed.' Yet he was still not sure what he should write after that sentence; possibly something referring to a basic principle of international law on human

---

* Arabic, meaning 'author'.

rights. At the same time, he was worried about an injured captive lodged somewhere in the ditches of that hill. For he was certain that, contrary to his intentions, the healthy PoW in the trench on the hillside had been shot dead by the soldier, who wasn't obeying an order from the corporal, but simply punishing the prisoner's 'crime' of expressing his delight during an airstrike against the back-up battalion. And now that the bilingual captive had taken such a hold on his imagination, how might it be possible to save him from death? So as he walked beside the prison camp officer, his mind was elsewhere. He was preoccupied with the trenches below Hill Zero, and with how many of the soldiers had ultimately survived, what their condition was and whether they had received any orders from headquarters. He was confused, and those two flies would not desist from their lovemaking, and the children … Ah, another candle; the last one has burnt out. By now, the cigarette packet is half-empty and here he is, still caught in the grip of a phrase that is both self-evident and aesthetically unappealing. Yes, of course, it stands to reason that prisoners must not be killed!

But … this old black telephone, which looks like something from the Second World War, with its insistent and monotonous bell which cannot be turned up or down, will start ringing. He is certain that, come the morning, at the start of office hours, its insistent ringing will abruptly burst in on the suffocating, damp, grim atmosphere of his sanctuary. Immediately after doing a head-count of the prisoners, this same voice, that of the prison camp commander, will be there on the end of the line, summoning him and

instructing him to wait for 'the same car to pick you up!'
And at the end of the call, he'll sign off by saying: '*wasallam
ya rais al-kottab!*'* And then he'll hang up. The prison camp
commander has never enquired about how he has spent the
night … because he has no idea either of what is going on
inside the katib's head or of what happened on Hill Zero,
or of the mental turmoil brought on by grappling with two
or three ideas at the same time. He has no real insight into
these – as he sees it – inconsequential matters that hold the
katib's mind so firmly in their thrall. A hill and a group of
soldiers whose task is to defend it, a healthy, young prisoner
whose life was extinguished in the instant it took to fire
a bullet, and his well-built body shoved into a pit at the
bottom of the hill. And then there's the other captive with
his fearful eyes and coloured headband that's still tied round
his forehead, soaked in blood and mud, so that the slogan
written on it is now largely illegible, especially in the inky
blackness of the trench at night. What's more, the prison
camp commander is completely unaware of the fate of the
people who prey on the author's mind, the only person who
knows what happened to them. He knows their fate alright,
but just hasn't yet been able to plot it properly. Then there's
that firing button, the green or red button – or is it a light,
easily flickable switch with a hand outstretched towards
it – or maybe there's a finger poised directly over the button,
waiting to press it? Also, the thought of that wandering
object going round and round like a nightmare in the night
in the mind of the author, and his concern about it flying

---

* Arabic, meaning 'Farewell, O Master of Writers!'

or ricocheting; that nightmare has drawn sweat from the brow of the man who has been flatteringly referred to as '*rais al-kottab*', the man whose eyes have been fixed on the two cavorting flies and whose mind is left mired in a sentence which would appear to signal the end of everything, not least the end of the piece of writing he embarked upon. The ending of the work's beginning. The ink and that phrase written on the paper have been dry for hours, but he's finding it impossible to venture beyond that point. Perhaps because he knows that the statement 'prisoners must not be killed' will be frowned upon and that he will be required to change it to 'We do not kill prisoners. But our enemies, on the other hand, etc. etc.', for he has already tried it out in spoken form and come to the conclusion that such a phrase is simply unacceptable to the mind of a military commander. And so it is that the author finds himself ensnared in the sentence he has written; the ink has long since dried and the comfortable fountain pen still nestles, unused, between the fingers of his right hand, while his left hand clutches a cigarette, as if he's idling, and his gaze is drawn towards the two flies, darting to and fro, occasionally landing on his daughter's cheek, or on his wife's hair, or buzzing around the noses of his other children, and for a while his gaze is fixed on the black telephone, a memento of some time around the Second World War, with its insistent ring whose volume cannot be controlled, and a thought rushes into his mind: to hell with this pen, this paper, this text and all publishers. Since time immemorial, we poets have assuaged and mollified the drunkenness of caliphs with our grandiloquent oratory and the tenderness of our temperament, to the accompaniment of the lute; and now we are expected to use our words to applaud and encourage the insane intoxication of our leaders, leaden words that have to march at the speed of a printing press, draped in military clothes and paraded in front of eyes that cannot stand seeing any bad news in print.

'Pretty as a bride, Katib! Look at their photos. I took them to the bath-house, to the barber's and then to the underground solitary confinement cell. I filmed them on the first night and recorded their confessions. Their sentences will be mitigated by these confessions. I've given them a promise, man to man, that I'll save them from being convicted at the trial. Because the way I've presented it, they were simply defending their honour – after all, two proud young men will naturally want to defend their characters in front of other prisoners! They say exactly the same things in the film. In it, they speak in fluent Arabic, because it's been four years since they were taken prisoner and when they were captured they can't even have been fifteen years old. I can show you the film so that you can see for yourself how easily and freely they speak. There are no signs of pressure or nerves on their faces, and no sign of violence. I extract confessions from every prisoner according to their individual temperament, age and beliefs. I find out the weaknesses of each person depending on their circumstances; and what are the weaknesses of two handsome and proud young men in a hellish situation like this? The answer is, the hope to be freed one day and to live their lives with pride for a long time to come!'

'So how come they agreed to plead guilty to the kind of accusation that was levelled against them in their confession? Won't such a confession undermine their self-belief?'

'No! Because in their own opinions, these young men have defended their characters and honour in one way or another, and consequently committed murder. A premeditated murder, carried out with whatever objects they could lay their hands on, at the exact time of the day when they were sure all the other prisoners would be asleep. And even if a person, or persons, happened to be awake, they pretended otherwise to allow the murder to be committed.'

'Why would they pretend to be asleep?'

'Because nobody liked the victim.'

'Why not? How is it possible for a group of people not to like one of their own?'

'So many questions, Mr Katib; and I've no wish to break your heart or, God forbid, disrespect you in any way. The story follows two distinct paths from here on in: what really happened, which you'd be well advised not to enquire about; and what I've already explained to you, at least in part, the rest of which I'm going to tell you now. Take a look at this photograph. It's of the victim. Neat and clean, with a shaven head and a tidy beard. He has been murdered in the prime of his life. I've put his *turbah** and prayer beads on his chest in this photo. As you can see for yourself! Now, I feel sure you're going to ask me how a prisoner can be so plump and hearty? I will tell you as much as I can – please don't press me further – but he was given an

---

* *Turbah* is a small clay tablet used by Shia Muslims during the daily prayers.

officer's ration. He was chosen as the prefect of his prison wing, so on the night of the murder, like any other night, he knew he didn't have to shave his beard, dry or …'

'Or with his face wet with urine from the buckets, in order to shave with one of the two dull razors!'

'Your attention to detail is beginning to intrigue me. Very well, I will pretend not to have heard what you are implying but merely add that the murdered man had permission from the prison camp to – if required – lead communal prayers and arrange certain ceremonies. Look, I don't have to tell you this, but I will anyway – you should know, in confidence, that the only way anyone listened to what he had to say was through coercion.'

'I see!'

'And what exactly is it that you see?'

'The truth of the story.'

'Just hang on a minute … I trusted you and explained a few facts to you in confidence. You know well enough that divulging military secrets in time of war is a serious offence. So, get this into your head: the 'truth of the story' is whatever the prison camp office chooses to tell journalists, authors, the Red Cross or any other busybody! And you, my friend, should just listen to the truth I'm impressing on you and take a good look at the face in this photo. Even after suffocation it's still recognisable. There's a short pamphlet written in his own hand, as well. I hope you don't suspect us of having any hand in writing it, or of imposing our view in it – no way! He was trying to pass it off as some sort of religious tract. We have a sample of his handwriting in our archives. We didn't prevent it from being written and we provided him with pen and paper, a standard procedure under human rights law. Go on – read it for yourself. Have a look at this little pamphlet. You have my permission. Go ahead and read it at your leisure! The president would like the main points of this pamphlet to be mentioned in your article. We attach the utmost importance to it, since it alone will provide damning evidence against our enemy. What do you think of it?'

'Indeed! You could easily have got yourself a job at homeland television, sir, no problem! I can see you preparing hours and hours of television for viewers to consume every month.'

'It's very kind of you to say so, *seyedi*.* After all, we do a bit of thinking too in our profession. It's rather taken for granted in this job!'

'Marvellous!'

'You're not being facetious, I hope?'

'Absolutely not … twisting the real motives behind an act of violence which has been carried out through the collective will, then fabricating reasons to turn a disaster into a desired outcome – that's what I call a truly inventive and artistic piece of work!'

'Well, I think so too. But what is key is that my version of the story is to the benefit of our country and detrimental to the enemy. By publicizing this story we can demoralize enemy troops. It's indicative of a servile state of mind, even in prison, with a written text as evidence! I don't expect promotion for myself, but if this event is well publicized

---

* Arabic, meaning 'sir'.

and broadcast by the public media, I'd hope that my – what shall we call it? – "creative input" might be acknowledged in some small way. And, of course, your pen would have the honour of recording all this!'

'My pen! Yes, of course!'

'Yes … I'm sure you're well aware that throughout our history, the pen and the sword have always been close companions.'

Sword, sword, sword … yes, the movements of the two flies begin to look a bit like swords too, as they criss-cross one another in the air – and then suddenly both of them land on the black telephone, and become invisible against its background. Sword and pen. It could be that, up until then, Katib had not paid much heed – or really focused his attention – on the colour of his fountain pen. Now he spent another moment contemplating his fountain pen and turning it between his fingers. Homeland! Homeland, he thought. And suddenly he remembered that he hadn't given any thought to where exactly the hill in his story was located in his native land. Hill Zero, Hill Zero. And the soldiers who had been ordered to defend the hill with their lives, how many had they been to start with and how many were left now? Seven, maybe, there were originally seven of them, he decided. He reckoned seven or even five men would be enough to defend a small hill, maybe even as few as three; and in this situation, when should he deploy the reinforcements that were waiting in the rear, still all standing and fully equipped? What was their situation right now? He felt lost. 'I'm confused, confused,' he muttered to himself. The two flies would not let him concentrate, and … he thought that he ought perhaps to describe a false dawn appearing behind Hill Zero, and in order to move on, finally, from that repetitive sentence that seemed to lose its meaning with every passing moment, a blot on a white surface, it occurred to him that he should fetch the bilingual captive out of the trench. Maybe he'd then be unshackled. Having thought that, the author immediately fell to wondering whether his pen might even be able to prevent the prisoner's death. And again he wiped the sweat off his brow with his colourful handkerchief and laid the tip of the fountain pen on the paper after the quotation mark and proceeded to write: 'thirst, hunger, the feeling of being threatened, and the jumpiness of men who for a long while have been digging foxholes into a hillside and repeatedly having to take cover while carrying full or empty flasks …' He reflected on the fact that it might not be clear from this whether they were still alive or not. What a dead end! And now I've completely lost track of my characters!

# 4

MEANWHILE, THIS IS THE SCENE that is played out on the other side of the border, on the slopes of the Alborz Mountains. Here we find another man, bent double, a man whose whole body is twisted, from his wrist to his neck and his back, so much so that he can't sit straight anymore, can't stand up straight anymore, and can't walk straight anymore. And as he opens his eyes today – like every other day – this man reflects that he is not, nor has he ever been, the kind of person who thinks much about what shoes and clothes he should put on. This man spends his nights considering and marvelling at the cultures of these two tribes and the blending of their languages, which gave voice to enmities, humiliations and disputes fomented on the one hand by the caliphs and their appointees and duly responded to on the other side by those who were intent on confronting the Abbasid caliphate. For instance, Ya'qub the coppersmith seized control of the area between Ahwaz and Baghdad.* Whereupon the caliph sent Ya'qub's brother Amr a missive, requesting that he withdraw from the border and settle in Neishabur, where he was to await a succession of gifts and presents from the caliph, including slaves and all the

---

* The figures named in this and the following paragraph were all early rebels against the encroachment of the Abbasid Caliphate into Persia. As such, their conflicts with the Baghdad-based authority prefigure the modern tension along the Iran–Iraq border.

other things that make life pleasant and worth living; and it seems as if the blood on that tract of land has never dried up, for the people on this side of the border have never accepted the presence of outsiders, and never will. It was always so, and so it shall remain. As a prime example of this attitude, there is a famous quotation from that most revered and cunning vizier, the grand Khwaja,* who once complained that 'no matter where you go, the Batenians are known by a different name or term; hence at every city and in every region they are called something else, though they all amount to the same thing: in Aleppo and Egypt they are called Ismaili; in Qom and Kashan and Tabaristan and Sabzevar, Sabii; and in Baghdad and Transoxiana and Qazni, Qarmati; in Kufa, Mobaraki; and in Basra, Ravandi and Borqa'i; and in Rey, Khalafi; in Gorgan, Mohammereh; in Damascus, Mobayyezeh; in Morocco, Saeedi; and in Lhasa and Bahrain, Jannabi; in Isfahan, Bateni; while they refer to themselves as Ta'limi or by other names. But whatever they are called, their sole intent is to confound the populace and cast them into a state of ignorance!'

It has also been said that 'the basis of the religious sects of Mazdakism and the Khurramites and Batenians are one and the same!' And that all this began with Abu Muslim, in the year 137 after the Hijra,† when Abu Ja'far Mansur Aldavaniq had Abu Muslim Khorasani assassinated. There was a man, Sunpadh by name, the overseer of Neishabur and a friend of Abu Muslim, who had elevated him and

---

* Khwaja Nizam al-Mulk Tusi.
† Circa AD 754.

bestowed upon him the title of commander-in-chief of the Zoroastrians. After Abu Muslim's death, this Sunpadh rebelled under the name of Khorramdin, which he inherited from the wife of Mazda Bamdadan. And those deeds, which the vizier Khwaja called 'sedition', all stemmed from him and kept happening at various locations under various names. And all these were directed at Baghdad, to debase and smear the name of whoever was the caliph there at the time. And now, isn't this just another link in the very same chain, which has simply surfaced in a different guise?

'Did you just say something?'

'No! Did you?'

'All I said was jamoo.'*

'Jamoo?'

'Yes, jamoo!'

'Why jamoo?'

'Jamoo, yes, jamoo … but someone was talking to himself. I heard him!'

'Maybe what you heard was someone saying jamoo… did you get the word jamoo from a book?'

'No, I can't even read. But I remember the name of our village as 'Jamoo'. It's not its real name. No matter how hard I try I can't recall its proper name. Just jamoo, jamoo! Only this word comes to my mind and then to my lips. Jamoo … jamoo … jamoo!'

'Where are you from? The south? The southern regions, right?'

---

*A nonsensical word.

'I'll have to think about that, I have to think a lot …
please, some water – isn't there any water? And this enemy
soldier, can't you untie his hand from mine? I can't breathe.
Please, Jamoo … let me untie my hand from his. I can't
take it anymore.'

'I told you to untie yourself a while ago!'

'I can't, I tried, but it won't budge!'

'It's better to be patient, much better, isn't it? Just try and
think of something pleasant!'

'I can't remember anything. I just told you so!'

'A dove, how about a dove? You can picture a dove, right?
I'll help you, think about a dove, a dove that used not to be
a dove at first. But that later turned into one!'

'Jamoo … jamoo … that's all I'm getting!'

'Use your brain, man! We're in a trench, the trench has
been dug into the heart of Hill Zero. This hill used to
belong to the enemy. It's been three nights and three days
since we took control. We don't have any water, our flasks
are empty; we've lost some of our men from this trench and
now it's just me and you and a prisoner, and we're waiting.
If you don't think for yourself you might lose control over
your actions and put yourself in the enemy's range, Jamoo!
Let me tell you this, not everyone turns into a dove. Think
how a valiant warrior can turn into a dove; open your
mind, be attentive! A false dawn has appeared and the sky
is inching towards daylight. Think of a dove, you might
have seen a dove once on the roof of your house, in the sky
above your village, right?'

'Jamoo … jamoo … jamoo …'

'Goddammit! What about a lion, then, a female lion;

think of that lioness who might come to us – anytime now, come and find us. You know they call her the 'lion of the desert', roaming the wasteland to offer her milk to the thirsty and the distressed? That lioness; you must recall the lioness? Everyone at the border knows about her, friend and foe alike. No one dares shoot her, because if you do your finger will stick to the trigger and the rifle butt will burst into flames in your hand. The lioness looks at friends and foes in the same way. Blessed be the milk of her breasts, which are like a mother's breasts; a spring that never dries up. Think of her, think of the breasts of the lioness, bursting with milk. She roams the desert in search of thirsty people; she goes in search of the fallen. You should be able to think of her, surely! You've heard stories about her, everybody has. A lioness? Doesn't it remind you of anything, this image, the picture that's painted by this description?'

'Jamoo …'

'Someone is speaking to me, can you hear it? Isn't anyone speaking to you? Can't you hear it? Can't you hear anything?'

'Jamoo …'

'And you, soldier? *Anta? La Asmaa?* Anything?'*

'*Atash … al-atash ya mola!*'†

'But I … I … what strange loneliness! And silence … this silence … this silence! Disaster always follows silence. The enemy lies in wait at six o'clock. Advancing, its tanks will be blown up by our land mines; in retreat they can't

---

*Arabic, meaning 'You? Can't you hear?'
†Arabic, meaning 'Thirst … thirst, O sir!'

help but drive over the corpses of our men. So I have to focus on the enemy being shattered. I can only pray for destruction from the sky. I mustn't let my heart think for my brain! I must think like a warrior. Here I am a warrior. A fighter! I have to think of killing and not being killed. Once I've convinced myself that I'm a warrior, a fighter, then all I must think of is killing and not getting killed. When I declare myself a warrior, I separate myself from other aspects of my being. I won't refer to what I've read or to any prior knowledge, unless it's related to history. Just history; for history is the breeding-ground of crime, the blood-spattered arena of crime; and I mustn't let my heart get the better of my brain. They are killed, we are killed; that's all there is to it! But … I can't abandon this young man to the fatal thirst he's suffering from. My heart won't let me spare him a bullet and free myself from the weight of his presence on my conscience. It's heavy, it's weighing down on my soul, but I can't! Why can't I? Who would I have to answer to for it? Who is there to seek permission from? What guarantee is there that I'll stay alive myself under this hail of gunfire and fear? But if I can't spare him a bullet, I'm sure I'll keep suffering from this delusion that a pair of eyes is watching me the whole time. I can hear a voice, and see images … images; I see images in my sub-conscious. You! What about you, boy? Have you gone mute at the worst possible moment to lose your power of speech? What has happened to you all of a sudden? Maybe his blood has thickened and is not flowing to his brain prop-erly? Maybe … how can I know? Maybe that heavy bom-bardment that came down behind the hill has unsettled him and the shock of it … I don't know! He's so young, I'm talking to you kid, can you hear me? It's quiet everywhere, can you hear? Can you see the false dawn? Your eyes can see, can't they? Have you gone blind too? I told you the lioness was searching for us, I told you the lioness would find us. I told you that she feeds milk to the enemy captive as well. She doesn't differentiate between you and me and them, so just take care of yourself until she arrives. First she has to attend to the wounded, do you understand? Keep a grip on yourself. This is a battleground, a warzone, and you are a warrior! If you pull yourself together, I'll tell you how a human being can turn into a dove. A dove. A white dove. Do you understand what I'm saying?'

'Jamoo … jamoo … jamoo …'

'Put your hand down! Put your hand down, boy! Okay, then, I promise I'll personally untie your hand just as soon as I can. I'll free his hand from yours. But let's wait until it's light so I can see what I'm doing! Wait … I might send him to the trenches behind us. But right now I can't do anything, understand? Nothing! Just put your hand down! The boy's gone mad from thirst! What should I do with him? Patience, be patient boy! *Itikaf.* * Think you are in the meditative trance of *itikaf.* But stay alert! Give me your weapon. Quick! That's an order, give it here! I'm giving you an order. Quick! Point the muzzle down towards the ground. Very well, I'll keep it for you. I'll keep an eye on your captive too. Though there's no life left in him either.

---

* *Itikaf* is an Islamic practice consisting of dedicating oneself to a period of retreat in a mosque for the fulfillment of one's request from God.

Why don't you go and lie down for a bit? Get some rest! Have a quick catnap! You do understand this order, don't you? Take a nap while you're still on your feet then! As in with your eyes open! When it's time, I'll call you to attention with a punch! And don't repeat that word "jamoo" again, or I'll go crazy, which would be to no one's advantage. It will be bad! Very bad! Understood? So now lay your head on this clod of earth and lie down. You too, *anta*! Like two brothers. Until I figure out when this false dawn is going to break. My arms and legs are stiff … I must exercise them a bit … but … but … the sound … sound … what's that sound? I have to think, I must think, think. Someone once told me that you can get yourself out of a dead end by thinking. I mustn't succumb. I'll think … about … a woman…'

A woman, a young lady whose face gradually emerges from particles of light. A picture in a rectangular frame with a sky-blue background. She wears a black chador. She's young, her face tawny-white and beautiful. She has been mourning … she's still dressed in widow's weeds. There is no tremor in her voice, but she sounds unhappy all the same. She has no name. There are many widows whose names remain unknown. She speaks plainly, plainly and precisely. Always at night, it always happens in the night. The lady says it was at night that he arrived. He had waited until it was nighttime to return. He didn't want the neighbours to see him. He was wearing a uniform. His clothes were smeared with mud and dirt and here and there there were stains I could not identify. His clothes were stained with tar as well. His hair was unkempt. It was only from his brow, cheeks and eyes that I could identify him. When he came to the door, he just stood there. I looked at him enquiringly, why don't you come in? At this, he looked down, drawing my attention to his boots and the bottoms of his trousers. They were caked with mud and dirt up to his knees. I took his hand and told him I'd wash them for him … I led him into the room – at this point grief forces her to stop her narrative, yet still she remains composed. She swallows her sorrow in a moment of silence to prevent her eyes from welling up with tears. A glass of water is on a tray next to her. She takes a quick gulp, revealing nothing but a hand up to the wrist from under her chador, then she is ready to continue. Now the light particles have dispersed somewhat and the copper tray and the glass of water can be seen clearly, along with the cushion resting against the wall. All eyes remain transfixed and all ears sharpened to hear the simple story that is being recounted. Truth in its purest form is always simple. Now I realized why he had waited until late at night to come. He didn't want the neighbours to see him in this state. He said pretence is vulgar. He said there may be some people who could have gone to war but didn't. He said that one should not embarrass them. I sat down to untie the laces of his boots, but he wouldn't let me. He said he had the knack of untying them. I brought him his own clothes. When he took off his boots, he removed his socks too, picked them up and went to the bathroom and half-closed the door. I asked him to drop them in the laundry basket, I told him I'd wash them for him later. I heard him say, 'Alright, so you'll prepare something for us …' But he never completed his sentence by saying '… to eat'. Instead, he emerged that instant, without having showered, wearing his old civilian clothes, which were too big for him. He put on a pair of slippers and said he would be back soon, then went straight out of the door and I heard him close the courtyard gate halfway; he didn't close it completely. He knew he shouldn't speak of dinner. When I asked where he was going, he said he just had to deliver a message quickly. I knew even if he had a message to deliver he would have done so before coming home. I was on the point of saying to him that we could go to my mother's for dinner, but he was already gone. I don't know how much time passed before I came to my senses, took a plastic tub, placed it under the shower, poured some washing powder into it and waited for him to return to empty his pockets himself. Then I put the clothes in the tub to soak and started cleaning his boots and scraping away the tar that was stuck fast to their soles. I tossed his socks into the tub. How heavy his boots were from all the mud and tar stuck to them! I had to put a plug in the floor drain so the tar wouldn't get down the pipes and clog them. As a result, the bathroom floor became awash with black, tarry water. Once I'd scraped off as much muck as I could, I propped the boots against the bathroom wall, and that was when I caught sight of him through the narrow opening of the door, standing in the middle of the room, on the exact same spot where I'd been standing when he left. He seemed to be looking at his newly clean boots. I heard him say 'Come on, dinner will get cold!' There was a smell of kebabs and basil; I ran and spread a tablecloth on the floor. He said he'd been lucky to get there just in time, he had been the last customer and these were the last skewers. I didn't ask. I knew there was no money in the pockets of his own clothes. He hadn't touched the pockets of his uniform either, so … He looked at me and I at him and we both sat down to eat. He brought over a jug of water and glasses and I didn't like to ask why there had been so much tar and mud stuck to the soles and ankles of his boots. And he spoke little. Very little.

There was an explosion … Suddenly there was an explosion!

Dirt and sun and soldiers, the trench and the dirt and the sun and an explosion – the confused chatter of various automatic weapons, the sound of continuous firing from anti-aircraft guns, bodies blown into the air and ripped and torn apart, human frames, annihilation, instant craters. The film seems to be running so fast that it's impossible to estimate the time. Perhaps the entire duration of the explosion was just a few moments, maybe less than thirty seconds. And then a discourse begins on the heroism of a man, a young man whose wife thought he looked like an innocent child as he stood in the middle of the room holding bread and kebabs wrapped in newspaper. And the screen of imagination shows the face of a man who had a soft and sparse beard and tawny skin, a little too pale, and his gaze is so bland that he seems oblivious to the presence of the camera; he's about twenty-seven or twenty-eight years old. This is the same picture as the one that's propped up in a niche in the room, resting against the wall between two old tulip-shaped lamps. The colour slowly drains from the man's face and is replaced by the profile of the young woman, who fell silent at some point and who now resumes:

'I was startled by the sound of the explosion, but he remained silent. Then he murmured: "People's houses; have they no shame?" And saying this he stepped back from the tablecloth. It was the first or second year after the bombing of Tehran had begun. I didn't ask why he'd stepped back from the tablecloth. I assumed he'd just got used to eating very little at the front. While he prayed, I washed his clothes. During his ritual ablution before prayers he had asked me to empty his pockets. As I washed the uniform, filthy black water slopped over the side of the tub and spread over the bathroom floor. I washed them again, twice, three times. I heard him asking me to spread them out to dry, he didn't have much time. I realized then that he was leaving again early the next morning. I didn't ask "Why so early?" It occurred to me that he might have come here on a mission. Because in the darkness of the early morning, a car sounded its horn outside and he put on his still-damp uniform. I placed his boots next to his feet and watched him leaving from behind the window and saw the car. I saw him climb in and give me a wave.'

From the mid-point of the film on, the camera returns to focus on the tawny-white face of the man, panning all around him and giving the impression that he is smiling. At the same time, the young woman is asked a very forthright question: 'Was that the last time you saw your husband?' – 'Yes!' And then the interviewer says: 'If you don't want to answer this question, you're free not to. But if you're willing … then here it is: between two circumstances, two stances, two moments and, so to speak, two points in time, within a short space of each other, for example, between the moment he arrived and the moment he said goodbye and left, which was more pleasant? His coming or his going?'

The young woman hesitates, but the screen of illusions does not give her time for pause or reflection, for thinking or for choosing the best moment, making it clear that the film has been edited at this point. All we can hear is the woman's voice saying: 'Sorry, I didn't hear you! What was your question again?'

So he asks her again: 'And this meeting … was it your final farewell?'

The photo on the shelf seems to be smiling more broadly than ever and then we hear a voiceover of the woman's reply, played over a still image of the photograph of the man: 'Yes … that was the last time.'

Wailing, the sound of mourning and images of green and red flags, and ranks of young men marching out into the desert. And the headbands, red and green, that are tied round the teenagers' foreheads, like individual banners waving against the background of the earth and the monotonous desert, like a crescent moon torn into thousands of pieces, coloured in vivid green and red, moving patterns on the film's background.

And the sound of mourning and the rhythm of hands beating on chests …

'You never mentioned your husband's name?'

'No.'

'Would you like to tell us his name?'

'No.'
'May I ask why not?'
'He didn't have a name. He didn't want to have a name.'
'Can I ask why not?'
'You'd have to ask him yourself. He specified in his will that he wanted to remain anonymous.'
'Thank you.'
'Yes … thanks.'

# 5

'WELL, *SABAH AL-KHEIR YA KATIB!*[*] What have you done about the report? I've been asked for a response by my superiors. They heard about this incident, and I've been given to understand that we can feature it in our international homeland propaganda programme. The more luridly we present it, the better. It has attracted a good deal of attention, and it's important that material generated by us should catch the president's eye. It's a big deal; it could mean medals and honours for both you and us – drive a bit slower, will you, soldier! This gentleman isn't used to riding in an army jeep. Slow down, I want to give us more time to talk – I'm eager to hear, Abu Alaa, most anxious to hear what you have to say. I've vetoed any TV or radio coverage of the incident. Not just because of the presence of Red Cross and all that … how can I put it? It's because of the speed with which television's immediate images instantly evaporate from people's memories. I need a pen. The homeland is in need of your pen to record this incident. Even a short broadcast trailer to whet people's appetites would benefit from the magic of your pen. The homeland, the president and the people are proud of the enchanting power of your pen. You and I both know – you probably better than I – that we need an appropriate subject to whip

---

[*] Arabic, meaning 'Good Morning, author!'

up tribal and national sentiment. In the past, you have successfully touched on many different topics with your pen.
Whatever subject you've discussed has been a success. Of
course, those triumphs are testament to your genius. And
I personally have no doubt that this incident will furnish
you with another opportunity to display your prowess at
writing. Let's just say the raw material has been supplied
and is only waiting for a skilful chef to mix the ingredients
and cook the meal. Yes … an adept master-chef is what's
required now!'

'Why, thank you. I've been compared to lots of things,
but never to a chef.'

'I didn't mean to offend you, sir, really I didn't. I'm just
a soldier. Let me try another comparison. This one's more
appropriate, honestly. Imagine soldiers, officers, orderlies,
clerical units and artillery, combat regiments, infantry and
other units all ready and waiting for their commander to
issue the order to join together, form ranks, and march
in unison. In particular, it's vital that the artillery receives
clear orders so that it moves at the right time and to the
right place. Now, in this instance, you are the commander
and everyone's waiting on your command. You issue the
order with a sweep of your hand or by uttering the word
'Fight!' So, commander, tell me what strategy you have
devised for unleashing a story that I'm sure will explode
with all the force of a cannon shell when it's first broadcast?
This explosive round under your command, our historic
document, will be just one of the tens, even hundreds of
similar pieces of information that we plan to deploy to dis-
credit the enemy: a foe who fancies he has a monopoly on

virtue and integrity in this conflict. We'll target this supposed virtue and integrity of the enemy with your cannon, your pen! You'll be glad to hear – I may have mentioned it earlier – that I've extracted confessions from those inexperienced teenagers. I can play you their confession on videotape, or you can speak to them yourself if you prefer. But in any event, suffice to say that we've made history today.'

'Did you say *history*, Major? Did I hear you correctly?'

'Yes, history, you heard me right. We're engaged in another historic war with the enemy!'

'I'm delighted to learn that you're interested in history. Before this war, I was only concerned with contemporary news and stories. But for some time now I've been looking into the history of the tension between the Arabs and Iran. Of course, history usually reports animosities, wars and massacres, and ultimately, the defeat or victory of one of the sides involved. But on the margins of history, you come across some remarkable details that are worthy of note. So, a while ago, I decided to write a book that goes into all that history, all our victories and all the enemy's tribulations and defeats. In your opinion, Major, wouldn't that sort of work have a greater long-term impact?'

'Katib … Katib … we're talking as if we don't understand each other's language. Or is it that you can't hear me, or haven't listened to what I'm saying? Don't you feel the same way as me on this question? I'm speaking in Arabic and your dossier shows that you're an Arab, too. Unless your ancestors on your mother's side were Kurds – and you know it would be quite a black mark against you if that were the case. You see, if it were deemed necessary to do a bit of digging in your file, it could lead to your enforced exile from the homeland. To spell it out for you, at best you would be cast adrift in foreign lands like most of your colleagues, and you wouldn't be in such good shape as you are now. You get my meaning, I hope?'

'Yes, I understand you perfectly.'

'So let's return to our main subject, shall we, which is contemporary history. Current affairs, so to speak. We need your pen today. In the here and now. The past was what concerned our predecessors, but what concerns us is the present. The here and now. This very instant. Because it is quite possible that some Ajam* aircraft might just have taken off, and by chance, chosen to target this road along which I, you and this soldier here are travelling to reach our destination. What I mean is, we've now entered a war zone and from this point on anything could happen to us! We're in danger, do you understand? It's perfectly possible for a plane with a devil's apprentice of a pilot at the controls to slip under our radar by flying in at a low altitude and to suddenly appear above our heads. Those types of sorties are usually considered suicide missions. It is almost impossible for the plane and the pilot to return home unless by a miracle. It was one of those missions that destroyed our important barracks up in the north with a

---

*Arabic, meaning 'non-Arab'. Historically, the word was often used in a derogatory sense by Arabs to refer to foreigners who could not speak Arabic, much in the same way as the Greeks referred to other peoples as barbarians. The word Ajam, however, was especially used in reference to the Persians; indeed, the Arabs called Persia the 'Country of Ajams'. In the text, the word Ajam is used to refer to Iranians, in this somewhat derogatory sense.

huge payload of TNT. Displaying utter recklessness, the devilish pilot dropped his bombs on our barracks from the lowest possible altitude and then pulled his aircraft up like a *djinn* and high-tailed it out of there. I heard on the foreign news that the dreadful force of the explosion had shattered the windshield of his plane and burst the pilot's eardrums, and that he had been killed instantly! But the other son-of-a-devil, the co-pilot I mean, was able to regain control and bring the plane, which otherwise would surely have crashed, back to the nearest airbase and land it successfully. But such unorthodox tactics are not confined to bombing raids. Sometimes they do it simply to show off their firepower and piloting skill and courage. Sometimes they'll just empty their machine-gun magazine and soar upwards. But although it's just meant as a demonstration of their military might, there's nothing to stop one of those machine-gun rounds hitting a moving target purely by chance. Like us, for instance, just driving along like we are right now. That's the reason why not every departure also means a return. I'm sure you bade your wife and family farewell when you heard the jeep's horn outside. Am I right? You said goodbye to your family, correct? Yes? I can't hear you, speak up.'

'Yes, I said my goodbyes.'

'So you understand what I mean by contemporary history? This is it. When the soles of our feet are roasting on a griddle, we can't think of our barefoot ancestors who ran around aimlessly on hot desert sands, hollering, to God knows what purpose! Right now we must tend to the burning soles of the populace! You are one of us, and this soldier here has been sworn to silence. So I'll take the liberty of speaking frankly. Let me tell you, then, that on battlefields all over the country, we are facing endless waves of enemy troops, wave after wave! We kill and kill and kill. But no matter how many we mow down, they never stop coming. It's easy to imagine that we've made not the slightest impact on their troop numbers. These waves of soldiers turn all the normal principles of war on their head. We try and maintain the principles of a classic battlefield army, whereas they ... well, it seems like their strategy amounts to nothing but this: to dispense with all the traditional rules and principles in favour of martyring themselves.'

'Major, will you let me cite an example from history for you?'

'Go ahead! Speak louder so I can hear you. All this noise ... and the sound of the jeep's engine ... please continue!'

'It's a complete 180-degree turn in history, a *volte-face*! The method of warfare you're describing reminds me precisely of our own when we attacked and overran Persia! They had a classic army ranged against us, and we employed unorthodox tactics. If you can picture that period in your mind's eye, then your idea of people running about on hot desert sands would take on a new complexion, believe me. If that period had only been imprinted firmly on our collective memory, then you wouldn't be so surprised at the notion of waves of human beings so fanatical and furious that they can turn the principles of traditional warfare on their head and turn themselves into cannon fodder. For that reason I believe it's essential for me to create a work that recalls the insane courage that our ancestors displayed in combat. A work that could bear comparison with what was written in Iran's Khorasan province a thousand years ago, all in praise of heroes and warriors of old, though of course it would be impossible in this day and age to create an epic of such proportions. But we can do our best both to delve into the meaning of victory and conquest, and to discover how to defend ourselves now. Especially by studying the manner in which the Abbasids defended themselves with the help of some Iranian families against Iranian rebels. I'm minded to write such an epic, pure and simple. I can only look at history from this point of view. And if this work does come to fruition, I'm sure that our homeland, president and people will be pleased with it.'

'Katib … Katib … Katib … why not just think of the topic at hand as being a chapter of the same book you are busy crafting right now? Each story has a chapter of its own. This incident could have come from the past too, couldn't it?'

'Yes, indeed it could. As long as there is war, there are also atrocities!'

'I didn't hear what you said! Now there's the roar of aircraft engines too. Say it again!'

'I said, it's just like you say. Yes, it could be an old story too.'

'So, to return to the matter in hand, what would you like to see? Those young men and the corpse, or the film of them?'

'Neither!'

'I can't hear you, speak up!'

'I said whatever you wish.'

'The planes are coming. I told you they would. The anti-aircraft fire has started. Switch off the engine, soldier! Get out of the jeep quickly and walk away, Katib! Move! Give me your hand, man! Take your spectacles off your nose for a moment and lie down prone on your front. In the ditch. Burrow down into the earth if you can! Lie down, lie down. Dig in. Like that soldier's doing over there. Bastards! I hope they won't bomb those silos … not today, at least … They've no idea their own prisoners are being housed in the silos. They probably think they're aircraft shelters or storage depots. No! … not today at any price … You there, soldier! Lie on your back and tell me what height they're coming in at!'

'There's no sign of them, sir! I can't see them.'

'What about that engine noise? Can't you hear it?'

'It's way off … very far away. Too high. They must be flying very high.'

'Why did the anti-aircraft guns open up, then?'

'Our jets have taken off, sir.'

'How many?'

'Six units. I think they're off to intercept them.'

'I think so, too. Lie down, on your front. Lie down! You too, Katib, you too!'

'They've gone, sir. And the anti-aircraft fire has stopped.'

'They've gone, yes, Katib. So, now you've experienced what the enemy is like at first hand. What do you think now? Is there any room left for your ethical qualms? Let's get back in the jeep, soldier.'

'Prisoners … we had a few captives in the trench. They killed one. With a bullet through his temple. He was young, tall, and healthy; they killed him and threw his body out of the trench. He was heavy. He rolled and rolled and rolled all the way down to the bottom of the hill. On and on he rolled till I couldn't see him anymore. He was lost, lost. I didn't want to … I didn't want to … and now, the other one … there's another wounded man too, and he's even younger … I don't want anything to happen to him. I tried to … What truce? We've been on the offensive or defensive for centuries … No caliph on this side of Mesopotamia had any peace for fear of constant uprisings. Rebels sprouted out of the ground like grass, raised a flag and rode west-wards behind their commander, towards us. Their destination was Baghdad, home to the caliph at the time. Their base was in Ahwaz. They stayed there, rested, replenished their forces and started out for Baghdad again. The heart of the caliphate. The caliph was the target. Until eventually they fulfilled their plan. Ultimately, those fire-worshipping Zoroastrians planned to force-feed us the same thing we'd rammed down their throats. Yes, Major? What manner of thinking is this? I mean this way of looking at the enemy? Yes, Major?'

'Are you sure you're in your right mind, Katib?'

'Only the flies … the flies won't let me. I can put up with the candle smoke and the smell of damp … and all manner of deprivation and discomfort … but these flies. The flies mating, the trench and the wounded captive and now this … this thought that has forced me to live in the past. Think in the past. The dwellers of the Gobi desert were under our control. Whenever necessary we dispatched them to ride in and topple the government in Khorasan and seize control of the throne. The Samanids! They were mindful of their distinguished heritage and proceeded to foster culture and produce scientists and translators and analysts. But because they started putting down roots, we destroyed them from within, so effectively that the last in line blinded his heir before going insane. As I've said, the Samanids harboured a nostalgia for old Iran and built a city of seven interlinked castles, in the manner of Ctesiphon. This displeased us, so we decided to set our proxy army of desert dwellers on them. Because the Samanid court had become a hotbed of petty quarrels and covert and overt animosities and inter-necine feuding, each faction raised a banner and a clerk and a commander and an army against Baghdad. It was during one such conflict that the desert-dwelling emirs rose up against their own king, meaning that they became heretics. The emirs' uprising did not achieve its aim of killing the king and seizing the throne. But it did prompt the son of the Samanid ruler to usurp his father, who was arrested, imprisoned in an ancient castle and then murdered. At the same time, an order was issued to slaughter all those who were heretics, in their thousands … it must have been during that conflict that the poet laureate of the time was blinded, perhaps after a false accusation or on some other groundless pretext!'

'Such as?'

'For being too good-looking, reciting beautifully, or for the crime of playing instruments well … or even for seeing beautifully. For seeing beautifully, and for observing beauty. Do you know what we did to the women of Bukhara when we conquered the city? They were the most beautiful women of grand Khorasan! And do you know what we did to the people of Sistan? The victorious commander ordered the dead to be piled up and blankets spread over the heap, which was duly done. Then he ascended the hill of corpses step by step and stood on top in prayer. And it has been said that he had a clear voice and a tall frame, large teeth and a wide mouth … but a coppersmith's son surfaced in response to that pile some time later and set out on a journey to Baghdad to assassinate the caliph of the period. A city which the Iranians themselves had had a hand in building – unlike Damascus, which was built by the Romans. And their treason against themselves has been a blessing to us from God, for all eternity.'

'Soldier, where are we?'

'We're passing the prison camp, sir.'

'Passing? Turn around and drive back to my office.'

'Yes, sir.'

'Stop here, soldier! Run ahead of us and prepare some coffee, so the katib and I can stroll along after you at our leisure and find it ready when we arrive. I want you to feel at home here, Katib. It's safe here. We're under the protection of the International Red Cross. As you see, we've run up its flag above that tower. So we can walk along unhurriedly and calmly, and you'll have time to reflect and I will be able to focus my mind on my responsibilities and my work. Now, what were we talking about?'

'We were ranging far and wide. From Sistan to Khorasan, from Khorasan to Rey, Sepahan, Ahwaz, and from Ahwaz to Baghdad and back again. We were discussing the downfall of Saman, the Samanid dynasty, the power and the wisdom of caliphs, the deployment of the men from the Gobi desert, and finally we talked about Baghdad and the empire of our caliphs, which was ultimately defeated by the Ajams with the help of the Turks, after some eight centuries.'

'I actually meant our discussion from Thursday, after office hours. I didn't want to interrupt your fine speech … but certainly, if there's time I'd be interested in hearing those tales from you, in their historical order. So, before we come back to the topic in hand, please make a mental note that you have to tell me about two things. First, the treason of the Ajams, and second, the conquest of Sistan and the conqueror of Sistan and the rise of the coppersmith's son … and then, those women of Bukhara and that poet laureate … and … ah … well, the whole lot, basically … but let's go to my office now, drink the coffee the soldier has brewed for us, and talk turkey about what really happened. The murder of a prisoner at the hands of two fellow inmates, and a pamphlet left by the victim and the backgrounds of all those three, paying special attention to the time they spent together in prison. Please, after you!'

# 6

AND NOW ... SOMEWHERE a finger presses a button, a hand flicks a switch, and from a gaping metal maw a monster is released, soaring up under the dome of a sky that is blue, or maybe leaden, or perhaps cloudy and a bit rainy. But where is it bound for, this monster that flies yet which has no wings? No one knew the answer to this for sure, not even the owner of that hand or finger. By contrast, there were many who became aware of its sudden descent, but they don't exist anymore to tell the tale. The wide muzzle of that metal barrel still smells of hell. But you ... my son, Jamoo! Now be attentive! Open your mouth, grip my finger with your tongue between your lips and suck! Quick, before this life-giving sustenance goes to waste. It must be a bit salty, but it will save you from being overcome by faintness. Suck well, suck my finger, boy, harder, use more force. Just like a hungry child drinking from his mother's breast. Drink before you lose consciousness. Drink! I want you to come to your senses and convey a message for me. Drink, with all your might! Whatever's left over, I'll give to our captive. I don't want him to die either. Keep your wits about you! After drinking you must send a message. And if you're still dumb and dim and dense even after that, I'll bring you back to your senses with a slap! And if all else fails, then I'll expend a bullet on you even though I really don't want you to die. Quite the opposite, I want you to live. You must live. You're still too young to fade away. So ... tell me now, do you feel any better? Can you transmit the message? Now, *anta*! *Tashrab, tashrab!*\* See how eagerly he sucks, the rogue! Do you remember now? You couldn't wait for the lioness to come and find you! She would have come. She will come still. But for the time being just obey the order. Dial the code for headquarters. Now! Say 'Yes, sir'. Say 'Yes, sir', quick!

'Yes ... yes, commander!'

'Good, brave boy. Now transmit!'

'What's the message, commander?'

'A sea ... a sea ... the desert ... is a sea!† Done?'

'Yes ... yes, sir, but ...'

'But this, but that ...'

'Should I transmit that too?'

'No – of course not! Now tell me, how do you feel?'

'Better, sir.'

'All right, then, take out a piece of gauze, I mean a sterilized cloth, from the pocket of my backpack and bind my finger, not too tight. You can do it with your hand and teeth. Quick! I can't take my eyes off the damned hills in front of us. Let me see what you're doing. You can suck on it a bit more before binding it. Then I have some questions that you should be able to answer. Like what's your name,

---

\* Arabic, meaning 'You! Drink, drink!'

† Reference to the first line from a poem by Khaqani, a 12th-century Persian poet: 'The desert is a sea, the camel a ship, and Arabs waves / Waqese the border of the sea and Mecca its end in their eyes.' Waqese was one of the caravan stops on the way between Kufa and Mecca. The poem refers to the pleasantness of an otherwise harsh desert in the eyes of Hajj pilgrims.

where were you born, your parents' names … I want you to be as alert as you were the first night. Quick!'

'Yes, commander, but … why are you doing this, sir?'

'Bind it, the first thing to do is to tie it tight so it doesn't get infected. If it's infected I'll have to amputate it.'

'I've bound it … aha … and now another knot. Well?'

'I didn't want to be left alone. Now there are two … no, three of us. Isn't that better? And I've no use for a mute transmitter. Do you remember anything now?'

'Yes, sir.'

'Tell me, quickly.'

'A dove.'

'Go on.'

'We had doves in our house.'

'All right, was it you, your father, or …'

'My brother, yes, my brother.'

'His name … your brother's name?'

'Wait, let me think … on the edge of the roof … the doves sat on the edge of the roof …'

'Well … right … how fascinating! Tell me more – but take your time. Don't let your strength ebb away.'

'Wait a moment, did you give us your own blood?'

'Stop asking questions, boy! Haven't you realized yet that you're in the army and you mustn't question your commander? Think of the dove, your doves. I like birds, and doves better than most. God's angels appear on Earth in the form of doves. I used to like cockerels better in my adolescence. Cockfighting … I squeezed a drop of blood into my gamecock's throat and threw him into the pit. You haven't seen them fight, have you?'

'A drop of your own blood?'

'There you go asking questions again! Try thinking for a change … anyway, I came to like doves some time ago. A dove! I've told you a person can turn into a dove, right? Yes … you must remember. The first of them turned into a dove in Baghdad. Not very far from here … it isn't more than a few hours from Ahwaz to Baghdad if all the transport's running smoothly. He had set out from Ahwaz, too, with a large army. Check how our prisoner friend is doing?'

'Looks like he's sleeping.'

'Shake him, check that he's not dead.'

'He's breathing, still breathing. But … it looks like he's fainted.'

'Let him sleep, he must be tired. Look, can you lie down in my position here on your front and keep your eyes trained on that accursed hill so I can get up and stretch my legs for a bit?'

'My hand, it's tied to his. Could you possibly …'

'Yes, let me do something about that. I'm afraid I'll have to tie both of the young man's hands behind his back. It's a golden rule that you should never trust the enemy, even if he's incapacitated. Well, now he's lying on his belly, let him sleep. Let me see if you can solve this riddle while I'm taking a stroll.'

'What riddle's that?'

'Let me get my feet out of these boots before I tell you. I mustn't let the sound of my footsteps … ah, that's better! I meant the riddle of how humans turn into doves!'

The scouts' frontline trench can't have been very wide or long. A mere slit in the hillside; only just large enough for a person to fit into. Like a dagger slipping into its sheath, say. So if our commander was able to relieve his legs from numbness by taking just a few short, light steps, it was because his body was emaciated and he was not very tall to begin with. Even that tight ditch was a blessing for him, allowing him to take three or four steps forward and back and every now and then adjust the focus on the binoculars his trench-mate was looking through, as a pretext for keeping the young man from succumbing to sleep. For every night, no matter how interminable and uncomfortable, eventually gives way to day, when everything becomes clear. The arc of gunfire behind them had ceased for some time now. And on the other side, the flames and smoke beyond the far hill had also died down. The sound of alarms had abated as well, along with the din of ambulance sirens and armoured personnel carrier engines. Many plumes of smoke rose slowly and dispersed. The aircraft of both sides had done their job and were gone now; all that was left behind was the ambiguity surrounding both hills and the doubt of the soldiers occupying them. The distance between the two hills was not great. Barely wider than a narrow strait. Water … water was down there. A water tank nestling under the brow of the hill, behind an earthen rampart. So far, five men – yes, five – had gone to fetch water and not come back. They had crawled towards the tank as best they could, but they had been unable to make it back and each dead man was a burden of torment weighing down on the soul of this young man who did not want to retell the calamity, either to anyone else or to himself. Even his good humour, and his ordering around and browbeating of the young radio operator were thin dust-layers that he deliberately sprinkled on his internal scars.

A skilled enemy sniper was lurking on the far hill. The sound of an exploding water flask was proof of his good aim. Why hadn't I tried to dissuade the men? Of course, I couldn't do that. Thirst had driven them mad ... and exhibiting their courage and nobility was the very quest they had come to the desert to fulfil. Water-bearing was an act of heroism firmly etched on their minds. The lure of filling the flasks with water and dragging them back up the hill while at the very limit of their endurance, that was their one great desire; it helped them feel themselves worthy of the ideal they aspired to. What was I supposed to do in these circumstances? They – or at least some of them – were young volunteers and privates. 'Volunteer by all means!' I'd told them, but I'd been at pains to stress that it was every man's personal decision, and warned them of the slim chances of coming back alive ... what more could I have done? I suppose I could have ordered them to attempt a surprise attack by working around the flank of the hill and then storming the enemy trenches using all available means, but the enemy had the hills completely covered and within range of troops in the fields below. If the bombing had happened two nights ago and I still had all my men, maybe that might have been the only possible strategy. But the air support was two days and two nights' late, and a person's bodily fluids evaporate under this searing sun, which makes even snakes slide underground from thirst! And now, what can I do and what can I say?

'Do you know what gangrene is, boy?'

'Gangrene? Never heard of it, sir.'

'Gangrene means that your bones in your limbs start rotting. Like an arm or a leg. First it's injured, then the wound reaches the bone, the bone is infected, the infection spreads and if you can't stop it, eventually it will kill you. That's why they amputate a gangrenous arm or leg. I severed it. I cut away the gangrene!'

'Sir?'

'I mean I amputated the entire twenty-seven years of my life.'

'I don't understand, sir!'

'Forget it; see if you can spot any movement on that damned hill.'

'I don't see anything.'

'In this cul-de-sac, the winner is the one who manages to take the last breath.'

'What did you say, sir?'

'I was talking to myself about that lioness. I still don't think you believe that there really is such a lioness in this desert. I know ... yes, I know blood is salty. It will make you even more thirsty ... thirstier! But what can I do? Don't be shy, let me know the moment you think your strength is at an end. And another thing – if we're captured ... no ... focus your attention on that accursed hill! They've all travelled on the same path. All of my ancestors and yours! Right here, on this very spot. They rested in Ahwaz and raised their standard ...'

'Are you talking to me, sir?'

'No, son. You just keep your eyes on that hill. And they

all came from far-away regions and farther still! What mystery is this?'

'My heart … my heart … my heart.' This was the first time my heartbeat had escalated with such rapidity with the writing of each word. No, it wasn't a result of smoking the cigarette. It was the words that were to blame. Sucking blood, sucking from the gashed wound on a finger of a hand. Yes, it was at that point when my heart began to palpitate faster with every word I wrote. I could feel it happening, moment by moment. It was the first time; prior to this, such a thing had never happened. But I wasn't afraid. I didn't wake up any of my family. I had tranquillizers at hand. I put my pen down and stood up. I wasn't afraid, but at the same time I wasn't able to continue. The words were bursting my heart. The words must not kill me, the words are not permitted to take away my life. I stood up and reached for a glass of water without thinking. It didn't occur to me that my body might be dehydrated, and that a lot of blood had drained out of the wound on my finger. I stood up, took a gulp of water and straight away collapsed. I fell on my back and put my hand to my brow, my temple. What had struck me down so quickly and violently? Where was a doctor to explain what had happened to me? To reassure me that words aren't able to explode the brain of their author?

If this man, this side of the border and at the foothills of the Alborz Mountains, willed himself to take notes day and night, he would write in the same way I have and admit that the name 'dove' had calmed him down. Just the word 'dove', the writing of it and the way he could complete his sentence with this word have all probably ensured that his brain or heart wouldn't burst!

Once again a brief telephone call asking why hadn't I written anything about the war?

'But I have written something about the war – haven't you read it?'

'How? Where?'

'It's been published only once, maybe you were a child or a teenager back then.'

He pauses and asks: 'I mean fiction. A novel ...'

'Rest assured, I won't be late submitting it! But who am I speaking to, please?'

The person on the other end of the phone hangs up, and the line goes dead.

If this man at the foot of the Alborz wanted to write a diary, he should have kept a log of how many times he has had to answer such calls and what kind of answers he has given, but what can a person do who believes the entire business of existence in these times isn't worth the effort of detailed scrutiny, night or day?

'*Talie ... talie ...* in ancient times, a soldier in such a forward position would be called *talie.* The word *talie* derives ultimately from a word for the dawn, and by extension means 'vanguard', 'standard bearer', 'herald' or 'rider'. The *talie* probe the enemy's defences, right and left, while their own main army waits in the rear. They intercept potential deserters, mounted and with their blades drawn, ready to behead anyone fleeing the front. Oh you cowards! But *talie* also implies suddenly emerging in front of the enemy, like the night-rovers who penetrated the enemy camps. So here I am now, a *talie* who must not be seen. My banner is invisible and my flag is the earth into which I have burrowed so as to remain unobserved. But before I die, I must take down that skilful sniper. Show me the way, O dove! Angels materialize in your image. Reveal a path to me so that death makes me forget its petty meaning. But why do I feel as if my shoulders have been bound? In ancient hand-to-hand combat, the illusion of valour and chivalry was nothing but a veil to cover the abomination of slaughter. But now I must summon up strength of purpose, I must recall those acts of courage which this tract of land has no doubt witnessed on many occasions. Here, on this meadow and along these paths. I have no choice in this matter! But why do I feel as though my shoulders have been bound? Just like the shoulders of this unfortunate prisoner?'

'Well, well first lieutenant on duty, Abu Muslim, Laith Saffari, Babak Khorramdin, Qarmati, Sepid Jam-e, and Nakhshabi! O warrior! You're in deep! You've fallen into a trap that they set for wolves. You've been had, O you progenitor of all races and ideals, O wayward child of times present and past! Did you harbour naïve hopes or …'

'Are you teasing me, Dove? Mocking me?'

'No, I'm not teasing you. This is deadly serious.'

'I know.'

'A literal dead-end.'

'Yes … Every fibre of my body and brain tells me so.'

'So … what about you?'

'I still exist, Dove.'

'You haven't been incapacitated yet, then?'

'No, as you can see, I'm still here.'

'Being ... yes, you're a being. But it only takes a "non" to turn "being" into "non-being".'

'Are you trying to frighten me, Dove? I've read about, heard and seen the state of non-being with my own eyes. And I have not come from the desert of non-being just to be returned to it. You know I have taken the name of a bird. A bird cannot be destroyed, rather, a bird is *besmel*ed.* That is the non-being that we mentioned in the beginning together, you and I.'

'But you're thirsty, aren't you?'

'Yes ... and down there is water. A little hope perhaps?'

'It depends on how long you can survive in the name of "dove". And on how long it will be before you succumb to fatigue. You are, after all, made of skin and bones and nerves!'

'Dove ... dove ...'

'Daybreak is approaching, the infernal sun.'

'I will put an end to this before dawn, Dove, before the dawn arrives and sunlight appears!'

'Why don't you pay a visit to the neighbouring trench?'

'You've read my mind there. I'd thought of doing precisely that. I'll be there in a moment. I'm here to conquer,

---

* *Besmel* refers here to the supplication required in Islam before the sacrifice of any animal (known as the *besmellah*, or *bismillah*, meaning 'in the name of Allah'). The speed of the ritual is such that the animal (or person) is dead before the recitation can even be completed. The full incantation runs as follows: *Allah humma hada minka wa lak. Besmellah. Allah o Akbar.* ('O Allah, this [animal or sacrifice] is from You and for You. In the Name of Allah. Allah is the Greatest').

Bird, after all. I'm here to win a battle, so I don't have any other choice, do I? Death is my only option! The water tank is down there. In a secure location. I've lost five men already trying to get to the water tank. I have to fetch that water myself. I'll bring back all of the water bottles full. But ...'

'Yes. It is exactly as you see. The enemy troops were also seven in number, and now ...'

'Aaaaah! No doubt their lips are cracked and so is the skin on their hands. And their faces have all shed skin ... teenagers ... aaaah ... my young men ... is this how you were hushed up?'

'Yes, warrior! They got there sooner than you. They were quicker and braver. You can check their heartbeat with your ears. Maybe some of them still have a pulse.'

'Yes ... yes ... maybe water will be still useful.'

'It's much easier than bringing water up, and burying corpses is much harder than providing water ...'

'...or getting *besmel*ed while bringing water up. I don't want to die this easily, no! They've left their guns for me – my inheritance. And one of them is from a religious minority, he has two chains and plaques round his neck. Two! They all tore their collars in frustration, Dove. Suffocation ... When the blood can't make its way to the brain ... Ah ... if only I could wash the dust off them with a bottle of water. I will return, my men ... for the time being, I will borrow one or two weapons and these flasks. And you, my friend, put the receiver of the radio telephone back on its cradle, it's stuck in your hand. I will return ... I will return. You can count on it. We will see each other, either here or somewhere up there.

Bah … he can't even hear what I'm saying … his brain, with what little strength remains, receives the message, but his tongue is unable to speak. He cannot respond. Is it not so, Dove? Jamoo, wrap the soles of my feet in rags, will you! Quickly and skilfully. *Patak!** They call this *patak*! It's a winter binding for the feet. But if you don't want the sound of your footsteps to be heard, it can be useful in this season as well. Now take these – there's one, two, three sniper magazines for you. I want you to focus your fire on the spot where the shooting is coming from. And here is a machine-gun magazine in case our enemy loses his head and emerges firing from his foxhole. And now all that remains is our captive friend … let me see if his hands are tied securely enough behind his back. Tight. Yes, like that. I'll lay him face-down, on the hill, with his head pointing down the slope. I know … he'll puke up whatever's inside him. But there's nothing left in his stomach. What choice do I have other than to be cruel? We're taught never to assume that the enemy is weak. I'm taking these measures for your protection, Jamoo – Dove! You must remain alert and your mind must be calm. You do understand me, don't you? Answer by nodding your head if you understand, and if you can manage it, say something too, anything. Come on boy, dawn is breaking. We have to say goodbye! Say it … Dove!'

'Death. Have you ever thought deeply about death, Lieutenant?'

'If I ever find out why I was born, then maybe I'll also find the time to think about death, Dove.'

---

* Farsi, meaning 'small blanket'.

'No, really, I'm speaking in earnest, because it's perfectly possible that you won't come back.'

So I responded just as earnestly. 'Do you want me to go mad thinking about death before it comes? Why? Isn't it the case that the whole meaning of my life and death is summed up in my circling this damned hill, dragging myself up like a wild cat and eliminating the sniper whose eyes and hand never make mistakes? I'm only sorry I didn't make more of an effort to stop those five hot-headed young men. But in the suffocating atmosphere of the trench how could I simultaneously issue orders and obey them too? I wish at least one was left; that'd make it easier to take out that sniper, as we could crawl up both sides of that damned hill.'

'So now I find myself as the sixth man, and having no choice I set off to conquer. I've said farewell to the seventh, but … I will not say goodbye to you, Dove. Time is short. We'll see each other again up there.'

# 7

A KNOCK at the door!

It's late at night. Outside the door stands the major. In the background, the silhouette of a jeep can be seen, but this view is soon obstructed as the major steps inside, passing a folder from his left hand to his right, and with each movement the folder cries out quietly: do you see what you are doing to me, Katib? This folder is not allowed to be taken out of the military zone. It's a standing order. It belongs to the classified-secrets section ... it has a Red Crescent seal on it ... I argued the matter all day with Red Crescent officials and their idiotic interpreters! I can't keep the corpse in the morgue any longer. The case must be closed. Every incident has a certain amount of time allotted to it according to its importance, and no longer. So, finish the job, will you? I even escorted you into the military zone, which was strictly against the rules! I showed you the film, the confessions ... they've even been written down and documented. I showed you the culprits and left you alone to speak with them. What more do you want? Are you trying to suggest with your denial and this silence that what you've seen or heard is a lie? That I'm a liar who wants you to craft a lie? That the army is some kind of factory of lies? That I ... merely want a plain detailed report of my lie from you?

He has scared the flies away with the flapping of his hands and has robbed the family of their sleep, despite a curtain which was hastily drawn between the kitchen and the family's sleeping quarters when the major burst in. The katib tries to suppress his initial outrage at the major's midnight invasion of his house, to say nothing of that primitive man's aggression and bullying tone, which has no humane or ethical justification whatsoever. Which is why he has not yet lit the cigarette he's holding between his lips and is waiting for his adversary's fit of rage to subside; in the meantime he turns off the heat under the percolator, places the coffee pot, sugar, two cups and two teaspoons on a tray, and goes and stands in front of the major and says calmly: 'Let's go into the other room. There are candles there, and an ashtray … Let me bring some matches and cigarettes too. You won't be comfortable talking here. After you! No, no help required. I know the stairway better. I'm familiar with it. I've been living in this house for at least thirty years. Before the war and the compulsory blackout, the half-storey up there served as my office! I've glued black cardboard on the inside of the windows there, it's not terribly spacious, but it'll do for two people … yes … turn the doorknob and open the door … now if you can get the matches out of the pocket of my coat and … oh, you have a lighter? Even better! There are two candles on my desk. Thanks. Please take a seat wherever you like. A cup of coffee shouldn't do you any harm. It's clear to me that you don't sleep well at night, either. Or maybe the opposite, if so I can bring you a bowl of cool water. I have a small fridge up here; it runs on oil. You know, Major, people like me should never get married. But whether to marry or not is something that's not … not entirely a matter of free will. It's not subject to reason! That's both its advantage and disadvantage. After all ... how can I put it? Behaving logically all the time isn't very reasonable either. When I saw Sabrieh for the first time it was as if she was made for me and for my heart. It was only afterwards that I learnt she felt the same way when she clapped eyes on me. Isn't that weird? Isn't it strange that two people should experience the same feelings and affection for each other at exactly the same time? What's your take on human beings, Major? How do humans strike you? Are you aware that in our holy book, human beings have been called the most noble of creatures? "Noblest of all creation"! Do you agree with such an accolade?'

'What are you trying to say?'

'I mean, do you believe in the nobility of human beings, in the superiority of human beings over other creatures?'

'And what if I do?'

'What about the forgetfulness of human beings, the fact that humans are by nature forgetful creatures?'

'Of course, one forgets things more often than not. This is why pen and paper were invented, so that one can write down things that might otherwise get forgotten. I do the same. I jot down my daily tasks in this notebook here, and before doing my final chore of the day, or even while I'm still doing it, I tear out the sheet of paper and discard it. Just like I'm doing now. Coming to talk to you was my last entry for today. Now show me where I can throw away these pieces of paper.'

'In the basket, the basket next to my desk, which has kept filling and emptying again throughout my life as a writer. Before we get down to the matter in hand, though,

I'll quote from Socrates about the invention of pen and paper. Socrates claimed that from the moment writing was invented, mankind's memory began to fade! This claim has been proved right through experiment and experience. Indeed, Socrates himself was living proof of this theory, for he was a man of words. At the same time, if writing had never been invented, Socrates' words would never have come down to us, and if we'd never seen them in print they would have been forgotten! We were talking about forgetfulness just a moment ago, correct?'

'You were talking about it, certainly.'

'And enquiring – I was asking you a question, right?'

'Yes, and I told you in reply that we can overcome forgetfulness by writing.'

'But I didn't mean forgetting daily chores.'

'No, I didn't interpret it like that either.'

'Sure … but I meant something deeper, I was referring to habit.'

'Habit? Habit?!'

'Yes … habit. We get used to forgetfulness, so lying becomes a habit. Duplicity and hypocrisy become habits; conceit becomes a habit; habit itself even becomes a habit. Your coffee will get cold; please don't think I've read these phrases from a book, or books, and just memorized them.'

'No, I didn't assume that.'

'I see you're staring at the rows of books on the shelves. Of course, I know some passages from these books by heart. If you like, I'd be happy to recite them for you sometime. But I still haven't got to the point of my question. To my point about forgetfulness.'

'I want to hear the answer from you. In your own words.'

'How about we drink a glass or two first, Major? You're not on duty. Besides, you've made me as flustered as you are yourself. Agreed? Have you ever drunk with literary folk? Of course I'm a rather moderate drinker myself, because I'm not a poet and never was. But Arab poets – with whose names you'll no doubt be familiar – have discussed every topic there is, and wine was certainly the muse behind their poetic deeds and words; and in extreme cases, they even came to resemble those ancient lords who gave themselves over entirely to drinking and merriment. Though I'm not a poet, still I'll pour us some drinks. You've turned me into an insomniac, Major! Anyway, here's to joy!'

'To joy!'

'And now let's have another one ... and after the third glass I'll tell you about forgetfulness, about what I meant and mean by forgetfulness! Enjoy! Praise be to his pure, fault-concealing regard!'*

'Which Arab poet wrote that?'

'I've forgotten now. I'll remember later. Let's drink together. There's a peculiar merit in drunkenness, which comes from the possibility of recovering the forgotten.'

'What did you just say? Recovering ... finding ... forgetting ... what?

'The possibility of recovering the forgotten.'

'Meaning?'

---

* Reference to a line from a poem by the 14th-century Persian poet Hafez: 'My master said there were no errors in the act of creation / Praise be to his pure fault-concealing regard'. This is a philosopher's response to his master's optimistic view of the world and its creation.

'It means that everything that human beings have forgotten in their long journey through life can or may be remembered. Usually one manages to remember in the end!'

'A long life? I'm not even forty-five yet!'

'Why, of course; youthfulness is written all over your face. In actual fact, I thought you hadn't passed forty! No, I was referring to the collective age of human beings, our chronological age … a historic forgetfulness!'

'I'm confused, Katib, you've baffled me! Come on, just spit it out and have done with it! I'm a soldier and being soldierly means being precise. Tell me precisely what you're trying to say.'

'Precision … yes, precision. But there was nothing vague in my speech when I spoke of habit. I say humans get used to habit, and forgetfulness becomes a habit for us. Skimming words, passing over words has become a habit for humans. Maybe if pen and paper hadn't been invented, humans would have developed a sharper capacity for memorizing words. For example, this title of the "noblest in creation" might have left a trace on the memory of mankind that was not superficial and shallow; that would not have been forgotten, and if uttered it would not be out of habit, and so this most important judgement on mankind would not be destroyed by mankind, and this accursed brain would not have dragged me to the edge of insanity, to a point where I have arrived at the horrendous conclusion that there is nothing in this world more vile, base, destructive and hypocritical than the clay of Adam … and my captive in the trench is thirsty, Major. Even monkeys don't take their own kind as captives …'

'Well, it's because …'

'I know, I know … it's a fact of life, but no less distressing for that, that if you don't take him captive, he will kill you! Forgive me, Major, for everyone has a child inside himself, and I'm no exception. You pour this time, Major, pour us another glass!'

'Are you alright, Katib?

'I'm fine, yes … couldn't be better. These flies … these flies are driving me mad! Can you see them? You can't? Down there, they were on the kitchen table, didn't you see them? All night long, dancing in front of my eyes … ah … my pen and fingers are both stiff and I stare at them, for hours and hours, staring, and I can't find a way towards salvation. I can't find a way. They perish from heat and thirst! Why don't you exterminate the city's insects, Major? Isn't everything under the army's command now? So why don't you turn your attention to public sanitation in the city? Pour … please do. Here's to joy! To revelry, Arab-style! But … what was I saying? Mankind … yes, human beings! I've come to the conclusion that God has turned his back on us humans. Turned his face away. Everything … we see everything as ugly and vile. We regard it all as destructive, ruinous, annihilating. Everyone is inflicted with the madness of annihilation. God has turned his back on mankind. The fact that God has turned his face away from human beings is the pet theory of this katib, Major. Mark my words. This is the theory of a Mesopotamian katib, a counter-theory to the famous dictum by that philosopher from the banks of Rhine, who wrote "God is dead". No, I maintain that God has turned away and humans have slipped their reins and are now on the rampage, destroying everything. Not only other forms of life, but their own kind as well … They perish in the desert, I can't do anything. They are thirsty … On the shores of the Bosphorus, the fringes of the central plateau, at the foot of Mount Dena … in spite of all the water in the Karkheh River, they are still thirsty. They perish. Sir … why haven't you touched your coffee? Will you allow me to drink your cup? Forgive me, Major, I'm drinking again … let's drink together. To joy!'

'To the joy of conquest! They have assured us we will drink wine once again in Nahavand. Once again! To the joy of conquest! We have conquered and we will conquer again, Katib, and in conquest it is only victory that matters and nothing else. I live or die for conquest and conquest alone. The blood of the Banu Quda'a tribe courses through my veins. The blood of centuries and epochs of bloody wars … We rode upon them and … you say the rest. Yes, you! Aren't you an Arab too?'

'Sword, sword, sword and blood. Severed heads … gaping chests … thirst and the dove. Why have I had the image of a dove in my mind for some time now … A dove flying across the sky of history and never finding a single wall or tower to sit upon? Isn't this Noah's dove, which is still flapping its wings in search of dry land? Flight … the flight of a dove … a breathless dove … conquest … shroud … word … words … forgetfulness … mind … habit … flies … why don't you smoke a cigarette, Major? At least use the lighter for me … or this match … or look, look … the desert is on fire. Have you seen the desert on fire before, the earth aflame … fire upon fire … look … look … I'm not a poet … I'm a moderate drinker … pour … one more, Major … I wish this darkness … I wish there was no darkness. A tavern … a coffee-house … why won't a missile blow up my house? Major?'

'Conquest … conquest … conquest, Katib! We conquer … I'm a moderate drinker too. I will build you a tavern … I'll have it built. I'll break down the doors! I'll command them to open the tavern's doors! I have a regiment at my command, no, a battalion! I am of the Banu Quda'a tribe and this Colt … this Colt is my tongue and my blade, Katib. I speak through the mouth of this thing that you see before you … tell me the address of your favourite tavern and get up! Now … let's go and drink …'

'Words … word … sentence … what pleasure there is in plunging into a pool of wine, Major? What pleasure! Caliph … caliph … caliphs of Baghdad and … Bring his head for me! That vizier's head, that Barmakid and his son!* That is, the head of his sister's legal husband. The head of Yahya's son … the vizier's head … the one whose father,

---

*The Barmakids were an influential family from Balkh in Bactria who attained positions of great power under the Abbasid caliphs of Baghdad. Barmak's son Khalid became vizier to the first Abbasid caliph, while Khalid's son Yahya was a key confederate of Harun al-Rashid, the fifth caliph. In turn, Yahya's son Fazl was made governor of the province of Khorasan (in modern Iran) and showed great benevolence in dealing with the people there. Yahya's other son, Ja'far, was appointed head of the caliphal bodyguard and manager of the postal service, the mints, and the textile factory. Later Harun al-Rashid's relationship with the Barmakids deteriorated due to unknown reasons and he had most of them arrested or killed. According to one legend Harun al-Rashid's anger was caused by Ja'far's secret marriage to the caliph's sister, Abbasa (Encyclopaedia Iranica).

Yahya, was the most trusted key-keeper of the caliph's harem. Bring his head to me this very night!'

'The caliph has demanded your head, O Grand Vizier!'

'I have guests and … see for yourself, Haris,* it is a special occasion!'

'I can see … All eminent Arabs and distinguished personages from the countries under our control … but the Commander of the Faithful has ordered it thus!'

'Any documentation … or a signet … or seal? An order must be in written form!'

'But he is in a nocturnal feast … there were no scribes. You do understand … the order came on a night of revelry!'

'What would you do if you were in my place, Haris? I have with me sword-wielders who are ready to serve. If you were in my place, would you surrender your head to the blade?'

'What can I do? I'm just carrying out an order. You are a vizier and a wise man, you think of something. I'm devastated too. I have this job and earn my living thanks to you. I'm grateful to you. But what am I to do?'

'We'll think of something on the way!'

'What should I do afterwards?'

'We'll see. The order was issued in a moment of rage. Before we reach the palace … maybe his wrath will abate. We will go together and stand outside the harem's curtains … I will remain there behind the curtains, standing back, and you will step inside. You will say you have severed Barmak's head from his body and ask for permission to

---

* Arabic, meaning 'guard'. *Mirharis* means 'head guard'.

present the head. On hearing this news, the caliph will react in one of two ways: either he will be angry at you for acting so precipitately, in which case he will call for your head, but before any blades can be unsheathed, I will enter and kiss the Commander of the Faithful's feet to prevent him from exercising retribution upon you, and this will be the best outcome of this accursed order. For my death would result in his issuing the order for your death as well, since the caliph of Muslims could not leave alive the murderer of Yahya's son. But if his anger doesn't abate and he insists on killing Barmak the vizier, he will ask you to bring the head to him! In which case I will be standing here ready for your blade. Beheading can happen in the blink of an eye. You'll come and fetch my head and put it on a tray and take it to him!'

'Now I step in.'

'But wait, let me tell you, alas ... I wish you were an expert in the Arabic language and with a silver tongue could recount the services rendered by the grand Barmaki family to Commander of the Faithful and the Abbasid dynasty! But this is not in your power, for I know that you are a man of the blade and blood and not a man of words! So go. Tell them you have collected the head of Barmak the vizier and heed what the caliph of the Muslims has to say in response. I will also listen to what he says. And the head of Yahya's son is ready for harvest, right here.'

'Soldier! Take us to Ben Khalaf tavern ... come on, man, you must have had a chance to take a quick catnap, so don't look so befuddled! Turn around ... use the alleys. We will enter through the tavern's backdoor. Tonight is another kind of night! Tell me, Katib, tell me the rest. Did the executioner take the Ajam's head off?'

'He has not yet returned. And the yelps and squeals of the women plunging into water stop me from hearing the Commander of the Faithful's voice. But ... I remember that in the same harem a marriage was contracted between Abbasa and Barmak, a curtain hanging between the two all the while. On condition that they were allowed only to speak and never to see each other! But they were in love, Abbasa in particular, who was infatuated with the beauty and accomplishments and intelligence of Barmak the vizier. And Barmak had fallen in love with Abbasa's voice, who while seated on the other side of the curtain read stories from the book of God to her brother. Barmak the vizier was always in the private company of Commander of the Faithful. Abbasa spoke eloquently and recited well. This pleased the caliph, who asked his sister to request something from him, to ask him for anything. Abbasa said she wanted Barmak the vizier. Very well! But only to speak to! Just to speak to? That was out of the question. Consummation? Yes ... Barmak's mother and father provided the opportunity for a secret consummation. Yahya the key-keeper opened the harem's doors, and Yahya's wife, on account of their previous friendship, welcomed Abbasa in her home. And Barmak is naturally allowed to visit his mother's house, is he not? It was there that the seed of the Barmakids grew in the womb of Abbasids!'

'And then what happened?'

'They set off on the Hajj pilgrimage for fear of the caliph's wrath. The infant was duly born in Mecca and crows brought the news to the caliph's ears. On hearing this, the caliph of the Muslims set out for Mecca. Doves informed Abbasa that her brother was on his way, whereupon she put the infant on the water and sent it to Aden. The caliph descended upon Abbasa's tent and looked into his sister's eyes. From her eyes, tears of pleasure and consummation and birth flowed upon the lap of fear. The caliph broke off the pilgrimage and returned to Baghdad, where he ordered the executioner to cut off Vizier Barmak's head and bring it to him.'

'On a tray, immediately!'

'This very instant, O Commander of the Faithful?'

'Did I hear correctly, O Emir? I am to bring you the head of Barmak the vizier this very instant? Right now?'

'You heard me correctly. This very instant, bring me that head, which is so full of ideas and wit, in this tub!'

'Did you hear, Vizier?'

'Yes. This, my head. Congratulations to my father and my mother, and my condolences to your wife and family, O Mirharis. Tonight we both become headless, since you will not live to see the light of morning either. So I have no messages for you to deliver! Dove … that dove will carry my message to people's hearts. In this city I observed the ancient Iranian ceremony of Norouz.'

'And that child, what was the fate of that child, Katib?'

'I am that child, Major!'

'You're the child?'

'I told you, Major. I told you a while ago, that there is a child inside people like me. What I write is what that child narrates. Do you understand me?'

'Yes, I do! So you're that very same Barmakid child, are you?'

'No, no, by "child" I don't mean a particular child. The child within me cannot do or say anything that is wrong … or write anything… how can I explain it? It cannot shoot a captive, that one who was shot and thrown out of the trench, that was out of the control of my inner child.'

'What captive? What shooting? What trench? Tonight is the night of forgetting … so let's drink again and walk in the dark until morning … and while we're walking, we'll talk in such a way that maybe we will begin to understand one another. To be honest, I haven't understood a single word of what you've said so far. I just assume you've been telling me a story that I have not the slightest recollection of. Not that I'm saying I've been robbed of my senses under the influence of alcohol and revelry. Not at all! But nothing else sticks in my mind, because it's focused on one subject, and one subject alone. And while this single subject remains unresolved, the only thing I can think of is that you have Ajam blood in your veins, namely that our katib is a descendant of Barmak, and so has Ajam sympathies. And so our katib's pro-Ajam prejudice is stopping him from writing and compiling a true account which agrees with our records! Did you pay attention to what I just said? Do you realize that wine does not have any effect on my brain? I wanted to speak with you in the most deserted alleyways of this old city so that you'd have no more opportunities to obfuscate or change the subject. If you don't imagine that I'm saying this while I'm fully conscious and alert, well then, let me recite the key dates from your dossier from memory, starting from when you were fifteen years old right up to today. You weren't even fifteen years old at the time of the Abd al-Karim coup d'état against the Faisal clan, isn't this right? And you – your entire family – were living in Alemare at the time. And you, a Barmakid teenager, became an ardent follower of Abd al-Karim!'

'Where are you taking me … this child? In which part of the city are we, you and I? In which alleyway or avenue?'

'We're in an empty street. You're utterly dishevelled and clutching a half-full bottle, and I'm gripping you under your arms so you won't fall headfirst into the gutter and hit your head against the pavement. I don't want you to get hurt, Katib. I must take you back home in good health. The soldier has been dismissed, he'll go off and sleep for an hour or so and come and pick us up early in the morning, when we'll all drive together to my base at the detention centre. I wish we could conclude our business tomorrow, Katib. I've been entrusted with this responsibility and I have taken it upon myself to discharge it to the best of my ability. Now it's you who must choose between me and our foe, between our homeland and our enemy. Maybe you'd like to read an Arabic translation of some Ajam sonnets to me until daybreak; or you might see fit to quiz me on the topic that you've been detailed to record and write about. Or why not try asking me about any details that you're still unclear on. As you can see, I'm wide awake and in a good mood and in the magazine of my pistol – I say this just so that you know – I only have one bullet whose time and place of discharge is in my complete control! And now we're in a familiar part of town, the katib alley. And the door of your house is still half closed. We must appreciate the value of security and authority. You will not deny a guest entry, will you? There isn't much time left and I can climb the stairs quietly, and with your permission I will lie down for an hour on this bench next to your bookshelf. Watch your step, let me bring this bottle for you. Thank you!'

'But … but … I intended to use a white flag … I mean a shirt tied to the top of a stick, and so solve the problem of thirst for both sides. The same trench … the same lonely captive … I was planning to persuade the corporal to stop being so stubborn … to take seriously the threat of dying beneath tomorrow's infernal sun and … realize that the forces to our rear – what's the proper term for them? That's it, back-up forces – have been annihilated and gone up in smoke … that the enemy has exacted vengeance and these, these two arid hills are only occupied by two advance scouting parties from each side, and there is no way out for either of them. In any event, until a new military strategy is devised there is no way out. For them, a dead-end has presented itself and they have to think of a solution … find a way to reach the water tank, before it is destroyed by a wayward shell. Why can't you understand? Either someone must come to their aid, or they must think of a plan to save themselves or else … they will perish! So what becomes of individual wisdom and resourcefulness in combat? What would you have done, Major? What would you do when your communication lines are cut, when behind you everything is in ruins and it's been seventy-two hours since any water has entered the soldiers' bodies? When one after another they succumb to dizziness and fainting and death? Why won't your obstinate corporal do something? Why has he pinned his hopes on the chance that his bullet will find its target if the enemy goes mad from thirst and charges out of the trench in the direction of the water tank? He's insane, isn't he? Why don't you desist from this madness? The enemy has lost five men for the sake of water. No commander, whoever he is, would allow the sixth person to be sacrificed trying and failing to reach the water tank. No doubt he will look for another solution and seek another strategy and ... killing that sole captive will not provide an answer to the corporal's problem! The idea that I have, my scheme, is that the remaining captive should take off his shirt and tie it to the top of a stick. He then advances towards the water tank, with the flasks wrapped around his neck like a collar. What do you think, Major? Huh? That way, maybe the other side would respond in kind and send out one of their prisoners to do the same. A white shirt on a stick, what do you reckon? They'd live ... all those still remaining would survive. This one-off action in such a dire emergency can't be against the rules, Major, can it? Well? Has sleep taken hold of you, then? Right! So who have I been talking to all this time? Myself, it seems! You might have thought about leaving me in peace in the first place so I could have got on with my writing! It's gone now, though, my urge to put pen to paper! Why don't you leave me be, oh ... curses upon everything that has distracted me! I was on a totally different plane of thought before you came along ... No, I mustn't even think such thoughts! Even if I had that pistol of yours with its single bullet in my hands, even if this wasn't my house, and I was sure that this portly figure snoring on my bench was my enemy, even then I couldn't bring myself to shoot. Not a chance. Even the knowledge that the bullet is waiting there in the magazine for me cannot make me commit murder! I fully understand his undisguised threats, but even so I prefer not to let the thought of murder enter my head. I'll just take that bottle out of his hands now; I'm sure he won't wake up. Easy does it ... yes, that's it. I could draw the pistol out of its holster just as easily and he wouldn't feel a thing! But I shudder at the thought of my hand grasping the butt of the gun, I really do! It is a vexing and irksome thought and I can't put it from my mind whenever I feel as though he has put his hand on mine, and is squeezing the pen between my fingers and compelling me to write about a subject whose truth is utterly remote from my imagination. The perverse story that he has concocted inspires nothing in me. They ... they came up with this plan themselves, I'm well aware, and arranged the whole thing. But they still want to publish it under my name and signature. Isn't that right, Major? Isn't that what you want?'

'Water ... water ... I want some water ... I'm thirsty, Katib. A sip of water!'

'Water, water here too!'

'And my pistol ... pistol!'

'Pistol ... pistol ... pistol!'

# 8

A PISTOL, YES! A pistol.

On this side of the border, on the lower slopes of the Alborz Mountains, the man who was smitten by words* had grasped the meaning of 'pistol' for the first time in the form of a slap, a pistol-whipping across his face. This was the first time he really came to comprehend the concept of *pistol*. A short time later, however, the meaning changed for him; when he read somewhere or heard it mentioned that *pistol* can mean a revolver, as well as an automatic handgun. The small and compact kind of gun was the one he'd seen in the hands of cinematic conquerors; whereas the larger, heavier and longer sort, strapped to the waist, directly above the right or sometimes above the left thigh, was the type used by Western conquerors in former times. A muzzle-loading rifle, a Hassan Musa rifle,† a Brno ... other names of this kind then came flooding into his empty mind. And after processing this information, it gradually dawned on him that, ever since the invention of lead bullets along with a device from which they could be fired in order to kill people, human beings have become nothing but statistics and can hardly be called 'people' anymore. And

---

*Refers to a poem by the 17th-century Persian poet, Saib Tabrizi. The first two lines of the poem translate to: 'when a person who is smitten by words is given a pen, he will not stop writing even if threatened by a blade.'

† A muzzle-loading rifle manufactured in Iran.

consequently, honour, kindness and humanity are now redundant concepts. For this new invention can be aimed and fired at anonymous individuals known as 'targets'.

Moreover, in his youth, when he was taking evening classes to study for his high-school exams – the exams for mature students – he would often see a man of about fifty in the exam hall, and the nervous twitching of his thick eyebrows, whether intentionally or not, kept shifting his round-brimmed hat back and forth on his forehead. This man, who always wore a three-piece suit with a waistcoat even in the height of summer, had a pistol strapped to his waist, a pistol that presumably should have remained concealed by the flap of his coat, especially in an educational environment. But that short-legged, burly man not only made no attempt to hide his gun, but every now and then, in a dramatic gesture, would move his hand and push back his jacket in order to deliberately expose the gun he wore strapped round his waist. Perhaps his intention was to instil fear in the teachers who held and supervised the exams. And perhaps the students of the night school as well, to intimidate them into not breathing a word or giving evidence about his blatant attempts to cheat!

In his youth, this author realised that this short-legged man was an employee of the defence ministry and that after his service in the armed forces, he was trying to obtain a high-school degree in order to increase his basic salary. But he didn't appear to have learnt any of the course he was being examined on. And let us suppose that, about twenty years later, the author saw another so-called firearm clearly with his own eyes. Not one, but two or three examples of the same gun. It was an automatic firearm, too. A machine gun! He was sitting on the back seat of a Paykan* between two young men, and as his eyes fell on the foot well in front of the front seat, he blurted out: 'Have you come to arrest Seyed Rashid then?† You should have telephoned; I would have come on my own!' They were young. The driver was young too. They didn't answer his question, so we can assume they weren't permitted to engage in conversation. They had their orders and they had to complete the task assigned to them. When he had come down the stairs to his office, he had taken them for clients or guests and extended his hand in greeting, and one of the young men had said: 'It will only take two minutes, sir!' and the other repeated: 'Yes, just two minutes!' I don't want to waste any time recounting what happened in those two minutes, as it will distract us from the main story – so, this author looked under the dashboard and saw another firearm propped up on two or three volumes of high school books. The weapon's butt was black. Like the books. 'Are you studying too? At evening classes, right?' he asked. 'Yes!' The only response he got was a 'yes', nothing more. At the junction, before the car could turn left towards the police station and, of course, that blind spot known as the Anti-Terror Joint Committee, the author enquired: 'In that case, will you let me buy a pack of cigarettes?' 'Yes, be our guest,' came the reply. None of them even bothered escorting him to the

---

*A saloon car produced in Iran from the late 1960s to the late 1990s, the Paykan was a licence built version of the British Hillman Hunter.
† A rebel during the reign of Reza Shah.

shop. One of them just stood by the open door of the car, and after that no more than two words were spoken during the journey, and not by the man, but by them.

'Beg your pardon. Please lower your head and blindfold yourself, sorry ... yes, that's it, use your own scarf, tie it over your eyes ...'

And then after getting out of the car, going through some metal doors and being led along by one of the two young guards, the same man whispered to him: 'Don't worry, sir, an innocent man has nothing to fear.' A genuine consolation. For this man was certain now that the matter was a serious one and that he had entered – or rather, was being led – into a labyrinth that it would take much longer than a matter of minutes to find his way out of. And so it turned out. It transpired that, later that same day, at sundown, the interrogator came in and slammed the evening newspaper down on the table, yelling: 'A peace treaty has been signed with Iraq. Now you're really up shit creek!' But that story is best left for another occasion. Our intention is to relate in detail a sequence of observations of firearms. In that blind spot, an interrogator was seen, who came to meet this author. He twirled his sidearm around his finger, like a movie star in a Western playing with or practising with his gun, no doubt parading himself and his weapon in front of this man, who had just that minute stepped into a concrete room, in a warehouse perhaps. As he entered, the young men accompanying him had untied the scarf from his eyes. The guards delivered their charge and then asked the interrogator: 'Will there be anything else, sir?' 'No', was the answer. The interrogator was a tall man, with an elongated and slightly crooked nose, and his face, as one might expect, was nervous and gaunt, ending in a sharp chin. Only later did this author find out what he was called.

Anyway … those two minutes lasted for two years, and during those two years, pistols, revolvers, machine guns, grenades, gunpowder and so on, were not mentioned by name but implied, and the accused, who had been apprehended in possession of a gun, was referred to as 'metallic, the guy's metallic', except on a special occasion, after the case had become public: 'I had my weapon at my waist and a cyanide capsule under my teeth. After drifting around for ages, finally I went back home. I ate food at coffee-houses with the capsule between my teeth. The capsule was there that morning too. Before I arrived at the front door of the house, I paused for a moment to tie my shoelaces. Checked both sides of the alley. Saw no suspicious signs. Didn't sense anything wrong. The alley was quiet. Too quiet. It was morning, just before sunrise. Quiet, empty and quiet. Suddenly a strange sense of unease came over me. I wanted to turn back, but I couldn't. I don't know why. Maybe because I was right outside the front door by then. An old house … it had a courtyard. A small shallow pool stood in the middle of the yard. I pretended to be tying my shoe-laces, placed my hand on my gun again and the capsule … I lodged it between two molars and … eventually inserted the key into the keyhole and opened the door, stepped into the corridor … didn't close the door behind me. Left it slightly ajar. My knees … my knees trembled involuntarily. The trembling came from inside, from hunger and a lack of proper food ... yes ... I'd become weak. But the trembling of my knees ... no, it wasn't really from weakness. I tried to steel myself by walking straight from the mouth of the corridor to the pool. Although I was exhausted, I didn't go straight to my own room, open the door and drop on my bed. Instead, I went to the pool. Thought I'd splash some water on my hands and face and try and stay awake. Remain conscious, so to speak. I grabbed the knees of my trousers and pulled them up so that the water in the footbath wouldn't make them wet, and sat down. I dipped my hand into the water, dabbled my fingers in it and then with both hands scooped some up and splashed it on my face – when all of a sudden ... I don't know whose hands and fingers clasped my jaws and mouth like a vice and wrenched them open, wide open! I felt like my upper and lower jaws were being torn apart all the way up to my ears. My ears ... I thought I'd gone deaf and there was a searing pain in my brain. I noticed then that a different hand had grabbed my tongue and was poking its fingers around my mouth in search of the capsule, and I heard him say 'He's swallowed it, Mother ...' and then I heard the sound of my sidearm falling on the floor of the courtyard as they held my legs and dangled me upside down. Someone kicked my stomach to make me throw up. My hands couldn't reach the ground and I don't know how many they were, but they had quite deliberately not grabbed hold of my hands, so that I was free to thrash about all the more violently, and try and touch the ground with my fingertips, which I couldn't, and all the time the kicking continued ... I didn't understand, I couldn't comprehend anything, and in that moment – I couldn't tell you whether it was a moment or a century – all I had time to do was to beg God just once, beg God fervently from the bottom of my heart to please let the capsule dissolve. But it wouldn't dissolve that easily, it wasn't designed to do so. It was manufactured in such a way as to prevent it from dissolving quickly. So it could stay under the tongue and last for fifteen or twenty days. It was designed to be crushed between the teeth, and I still wonder how they managed to pounce on me so quickly, how many they were and how they managed to deprive me of an opportunity to close my mouth! I'd practised it at least a thousand times beforehand. Practised so that it had become a habit. But in that instant, perhaps just before my upper jaw could move and bite down, their claws … blood pressured my head and my eyes, so that I thought they would explode then and there, when I heard a voice saying: 'It's here! Intact!' They threw me on the ground – like a corpse – and bent over the hand that had wiped the bile and the contents of my stomach off the capsule with a tissue. I could feel the sole of someone's shoe on my chest and hear voices ringing inside the bowl of my head and at the very bottom of my mind a thought flickered, of torture, of how long I would last under torture. Days or hours? And one of them had definitely seen my sidearm earlier and grabbed it!'

They killed him too. The final time they summoned him. How untimely! His fellow inmates looked knowingly at each other. They asked him to pack his belongings. Then they said no, you can leave your belongings here! And took him away. How untimely! And there was a reflective silence beneath a streak of sunlight which would pass over the floor, and reach the wall, and end there. Tehran is always luminous in Ordibehesht.* That day was luminous, too. Soon afterwards he was killed, at the foot of the Alborz … or on the slope of a hill overgrown with plants, surrendered to metallic muzzles. What sort of things could have been said? What pretext was there for conversation at the time of firing? Nothing was revealed to any of them, right up to the moment they ceased to exist. Because their eyes were covered and their hands were no doubt bound. Maybe under the hail of bullets each person felt that he was not alone and that others existed in the prison's environs, so that it could resound in the prison or prisons that they were nine, or seven, the number of the days of creation. The end. But where and from whose mouth was it heard that a severed head cannot speak?

This was the impression that man had of what goes by the name of a sidearm, revolver or pistol. But the firing of a bullet had not as yet been etched on his mind. Despite the fact that once, a long time ago, he'd been in a barber's shop when a man came in straight after carrying out a death sentence. Standing in front of the mirror by the sink, washing his hands and his face after a haircut and a shave, the man calmly announced to the shop that he'd just shot someone before coming there. He had a large, meaty head and his neck was short and thick, but not to the extent

---

*Ordibehesht is the Iranian calendar's second month. It begins in late April and ends in May. It has thirty-one days.

that one could say his head was glued to his shoulders. His shoulders would have appeared to be a normal size if his head had not been so big and his neck so short, and if his legs had not been too short for his torso. But the fact remained that they were. When you looked from behind at the way he walked you could see that his left leg arched in a slight limp; yet none of these characteristics could be regarded as peculiar to those who, throughout history, have traditionally performed the role of executioner. So, bold as brass, he said: 'I shot some men before coming here,' and added: 'One of them soiled himself before the execution, but not Teyeb!'* The man had performed an execution and then come along to the barber's, had his hair cut and beard shaved, and now he was leaving the shop again to go home. Master Taqi maintained a professional smile on his lips as he responded to his farewell, waiting until he was out on the pavement before saying: 'He's a relative of ours, the bastard! Warrant officer, forever a warrant officer!' and then asking: 'What day of the month is it?'

Then came the revolution and the sound of gunfire, and the rumour went round that you could get hold of a gun on street corners: a Colt, for 500 Tomans.† Response: I don't want to see its nasty shape. Or the shape of any weapon. Then there was the war and the newspapers were filled with new names and reports. The television screen was filled with images streaming in the dust rising from

---

*Teyeb Haj Rezaei.
† A Toman is an Iranian currency unit. 1 Toman is the equivalent of 10 Iranian Rials.

marching feet, dust rising from beneath wheels and vehicles, wave after wave, as they advanced towards the south and the west of the country. Once again they had to set up extensive networks of defensive lines at the border, organize themselves, dig trenches, stand and defend their positions – attack – patrol – get torn to pieces and … martyrdom. Green and crimson and black banners. As well as headbands, on which mottos were inscribed, tied round every forehead. Foreheads of various colours, the foreheads of many people, from diverse regions. So diverse that the five men who crawled down Hill Zero to fetch water and who were shot down each came from a different region. The sixth and the seventh also each came from a different region and province. And if this seventh, a lieutenant from the scouts' combat unit, managed to survive, he would no doubt have recorded the names and addresses and fates of each of his subordinates. Also the manner of their deaths and why they had happened:

It was beyond my control, sir! Utter thirst, pressure and despair drive a person to the brink of madness! Drinking water was there in the tank, no more than a thousand feet away, and the soldiers' lips had split from thirst. The skin of their faces was cracked and if they had not charged down towards the water they would still have become martyrs. There was even the threat of quarrelling and discord spreading in the trench. But ultimately they endured their plight like men and never showed any sign of weakness. Not even when they were starving – but thirst … it cannot be endured, sir! Water was within reach, but …

And … I am the seventh. I stationed the sixth behind the machine gun with the little strength that was left in him, and I went off to conquer. If only I'd had just two men, two fresh soldiers. Or at least one, so that I could have distracted the enemy sniper and created a diversion, but I didn't!

'I didn't, sir! The back-up forces were depleted too and dispersed all over the place. They had been hit by enemy fire. Don't make me describe it. The only people left were myself, a teenager who had been struck dumb and in all probability paralyzed, and a prisoner whose existence was nothing but an encumbrance. Time and again I wanted to put him out of his misery, but I couldn't. The military code of conduct did not permit it and besides, personally I couldn't, I just couldn't! Suppose he was perishing from thirst too in that southern heat, where it's so hot not even a snake pokes its head out above ground. Please let me have a gulp of water … could you ask them to bring a drop of water for me, sir? Afterwards I will be able to recount in detail the temperament, behaviour and even the words that my soldiers spoke throughout the entire mission. Name and surname, enrolment number and the methods of the action and reaction of each have been engraved in my mind. I was fond of them all. They had volunteered for the mission and none of them disobeyed me at any stage. They never came up short. But thirst, sir!'

'What about you?'

'It's not even clear that I'm alive yet!'

'What if you have survived?'

'In that case, I just declared that I will describe my unit's mission in detail.'

'This is a court martial. Do you understand?'

'Yes, sir!'

'So answer the question! You … Lieutenant in command, how did you deal with your own thirst?'

'Me? I can turn into a dove, sir! I told you before.'

'A dove? I've never heard of such a thing!'

'I turned into my name. I can do it. Doves are *besmel*ed, sir. Haven't you heard?'

'Take him away … take him to the lunatic asylum …'

They don't believe it. But I did it, I will do it. My old man turned into a dove, father, father, father, father, again my father, father, father, when he was released from his blood-drenched body … they don't believe it. They don't believe in taking off one's boots, wrapping one's feet in sheets, becoming light and flying. Jamoo … Jamoo … Jamoo … I want you to remain behind the shelter of this machine gun, don't blink, keep your eyes glued to that spot from where bullets were fired through the slit between the sandbags. Five shots were fired, and all five of our men were hit. All those men who went down there, one by one, craving water, and intending to bring some water back for you and me and this captive too. Concentrate on that very spot! Answer me by nodding your head if you understand what I'm saying!'

'Jamoo!'

Now he will pray for me, I know. I didn't ask him to, but I know that he will. By force of habit, under his breath. This is an innate habit, a sign of the loneliness of the children of

Adam. I become lighter, very light. Lighter than the soul, I fly into the half-light of dawn. I will not advance directly towards the enemy. I will outflank them. I will manoeuvre from Hill Zero and make for the wisps of smoke still rising from the ruins of their gun emplacements. Against a backdrop of heavy and light smoke, I lose colour and I take on colour. I move up the base of the hill. I have transformed myself. For a moment, the noise of a shot petrifies me. Then I recognize the sound as friendly machine-gun fire. Is it Jamoo? Why? I turn into a serpent and hold my head high. A serpent! Yes, I was correct, Jamoo has fired in the direction of the enemy trench. Maybe he saw a movement? That must be the case. Someone's head has peeked out from behind the trench and Jamoo has opened fire. But why should anyone have raised their head? Water. Yes, of course, water. Now a piece of cloth, off-white in colour, rises up from behind the shelter of the trench. Slowly, a piece of cloth on a stick appears and Jamoo gives no quarter. I hear a voice speaking in my language: 'Don't shoot!' And suddenly I catch sight of the back of a naked torso in the enemy trench. What a low trick! A prisoner from our side has been turned into a human shield against our fire. Blood fills my eyes and I pray to God that the teenager I've left behind the machine gun has come to his senses and will recognize one of our own men! But no! His sole focus is on obeying my order to the letter. But as long as our soldier is not pushed out of the trench, this in itself provides me with the ideal opportunity to act. I have to make it over to the trench instantly, which I manage. At this, the enemy soldier who has killed my five men starts spitting and cursing at us. And in that frenzied state, he shoves the muzzle of his gun between the naked shoulder-blades of his captive and announces 'I'll count to ten and your mother will mourn you if you don't step out of the trench immediately and order that machine gun on the opposite hill to cease fire'. But when he comes to *saba'a*,* he suddenly feels the tip of my bayonet on his spine and the steel muzzle of the sidearm which I have jammed behind his ear. I order the prisoner: 'Take his gun and obey my commands, soldier!' He turns around and takes the gun. Neither of us has the strength to fight and grapple in the trench. Nor, in the current circumstances, would it be to the enemy sergeant's – or is he a corporal? – advantage to challenge my position. My bayonet is already out of its scabbard, while his knife isn't. There are two of us and one of him. Of course, he is burlier and stronger, but he's also more tired. Hunger and thirst haven't treated him any better than us. I have no wish to humiliate him. I withdraw a step. I take the confiscated gun from the enemy soldier, toss a wire at our captive and order him to tie our prisoner's thumbs together. 'Tightly, boy, tightly! Now his wrists.' I think about saying something facetious to the enemy soldier, but I'm in no mood for jesting. I've exhausted all my energy in rushing this position and now he – whoever he is – is my captive, our captive. I call out and step out of the trench. Jamoo has seen my signal and recognized it. A mirror reflecting the light. Now the sun has risen in the east.

---

* Arabic for 'seven'.

# 9

'VERY WELL, KATIB. So you said you are the son of the son of the son of … that child whose seed was created around a thousand years ago in Baghdad, at the house of the vizier's mother, in secret, and who was born in Mecca and entrusted, in infancy, to special wet nurses beyond the reach of the caliph, the child's uncle, until he was taken to Yemen so as to be out of reach of the caliph's wrath, which could result in nothing but death? So you are the fruit of Ajam seed in the womb of an Arab woman, the seed of Barmak's son, Barmak! Which means that you must be a child of the children of Barmakids and Abbasids. How come there's no mention of this family tree in your dossier? You were educated in Cairo, and then for a spell in Beirut … before leaving to go to Europe. You studied French and history … anyway, after studying you returned to your homeland … and you are still alive! It says here in your dossier that you wrote articles in French under a pseudonym, which were translated under another pseudonym into English and published in Ireland! This is not incorrect, is it? I'm asking if this is true?'

'Yes, it is true. But it was a metaphor. I meant that my inner child has not yet suffocated in smoke and fire and hatred and gunpowder. But that doesn't mean that I am literally a child of that child!'

'I wonder! And what a night tonight is, Katib!'

'Hasn't it finished yet, then, Major?'

'And we're in your house again. In your room? And the good thing about the morning breeze is that it dispels drunkenness from your head. But drunkenness does have some advantages, even so; one says things one would not have said in a normal state. Perhaps you do not recall how the Barmak clan made a puppet out of the caliph? And that they dressed him in the garb of enemy princes and celebrated the Norouz ceremony in imitation of Iranian kings? There's no note in your dossier that you can speak the Ajam tongue! Where did you learn it? In Beirut or at Middle Eastern language classes?'

'What are you driving at, Major? Are you trying to connect me to the enemy through my kin, blood and tongue?'

'Everything I'm saying I've deduced from your own words, *seyedi*! I haven't added anything of my own.'

'I just told you a story, Major, that's all.'

'So you distracted me on purpose with a story to try and sidestep my accredited and documented report?'

'That document of yours will result in nothing but the humiliation of mankind!'

'It isn't supposed to result in anything of the kind. The be-all and end-all is the enemy's humiliation!'

'We have prisoners in the enemy's camps, too. How would you like it if the enemy started publishing similar reports targeted at our prisoners?'

'They have had no reservations in that regard! I'm interested to hear you call Iranians your enemies, though!'

'I've never claimed anything else. Haven't you read the

article I published on the morning after their missiles hit
our university dormitories? Didn't you read that?'

'I have it right here; in it, you suggest we find a way to
make peace!'

'I am a writer, Major, and writers cannot supply fuel
to wars. Especially a war whose meaning and purpose I
haven't yet fully grasped.'

'More, tell me more, go on!'

'I have nothing more to say. The sun has been up for
some time now. Of course, you are a guest in this house.
One should not set the time of a guest's departure. But
didn't you intend to go back to your base? Don't you have
a morning roll-call to attend to?'

'Yes, we do! According to you we probably borrowed
the custom of the morning inspection ceremony from the
Iranians, too!'

'I never said any such thing! Modern Middle Eastern
armies copied such military ceremonies from the West, as
did we. Its history is modern, not ancient. You can add that
to my dossier! I'm speaking plainly now – it's high time you
were gone, you're late for work, Major!'

'I *am* at work, right now, right here!'

'In my house?'

'Yes, sir! At work, on a special mission. I would like to
know once and for all whether or not you intend to write a
piece that faithfully records the information in that folder
which has been placed on your desk!'

'So you've come here to browbeat me! I'm very tired,
Major!'

'Surely no more tired than I am?'

'Yes, mental exhaustion, my brain is tired of absorbing and storing crimes! I intended to raise a white flag and at least in my own mind, call a temporary truce. But you wouldn't allow it, the enemy acted faster and the corporal of my mind was captured, just at the moment when the idea of peace had occurred to me. So he was taken captive, because utter thirst and fatigue had crushed his soul and forced him to surrender. You wouldn't let me do my own work!'

'Actually, that's not true. Your work is precisely what we want you to do: write, that is! The corporal has been captured, so what? He'll have to answer for that in person at his court martial. The subject I've suggested to you covers imprisonment as well. But you think the enemy is treating our prisoners with kid gloves!'

'Why do you insist on thinking for me, voicing your own thoughts and then attributing them to me? I didn't say, nor am I saying now, that the enemy is treating our prisoners leniently. I'm not talking about whether the enemy is kinder than us or not. My concern is the very concepts of kindness and cruelty. I am against the notion of cruelty, Major, and animosity. Please … before you leave put that book back in its proper place on the shelf of antique volumes. It took a lot of work to arrange those shelves!'

'How fortunate, then, that an Ajam missile hasn't landed in the vicinity of your house. If it had, you would become one with your precious books. The order in your library in an extension of the order in our republic. Now … before I say my final word, I'd like you to read a chapter of this book to me. I studied maths at school. I don't want to embarrass myself in front of you by reading an old Iranian text! It seems terribly convoluted to me. Even just skimming through it. Am I wrong? Here ... read this page. I've just found out that Iranians predict the future from books. Among the volumes that we've confiscated after overrunning their trenches, aside from the holy book there were also copies of Hafez's poetry. The book I want you to read for me is not Hafez. But ... no doubt any book has something to teach. So teach me something from this book, Katib! Read to me. Read this page, Katib. This writer was a servant of Baghdad too, correct?'

'Yes, it was written by that same vizier, the servant of Baghdad, and it contains a level and degree of fanaticism and hatred that compares with yours, concerning the enmity that arose among those people, and the hostility towards his sultan, and towards the caliph of his time as well!'

'Please read! From the beginning, from the part where Abu Muslim is killed!'

'But you asked me to read this page, Major.'

'And now I'm asking you to turn the page and read the passage about Abu Ja'far Budavaniq, dear friend!'

'... And so it was that Khorammeh, daughter to Faezeh, fled Madaen...'

'Further on! I want to hear about Abu Muslim's assassination!'

'...when Abu Ja'far Budavaniq, in Baghdad, assassinated Abu Muslim in the year of one hundred and thirty seven after the Hijra of Muhammad – Peace Be Upon Him – a chief there was in the city of Neishabur, his name Sunpadh, who with Abu Muslim had of old the right to converse and serve, and Abu Muslim had raised him and helped him advance to the level of commandership. After Abu Muslim was murdered, he departed and from Neishabur, with an army, descended upon Rey and stayed in Rey and as his forces became stronger he demanded vengeance for Abu Muslim's blood and proclaimed thus that he was Abu Muslim's envoy to the people of Iraq and Khorasan, bearing the message that "Abu Muslim is not dead…"'

'That's the passage! I wanted to show you the sort of people we're fighting against. These are the real children of the same Zoroastrians who have stolen our clothes and proclaimed themselves Muslims, while all the time trying to depose us!'

'But this is just a short account of a brief moment of history that has been turned into a story, and even this story clearly departs from the historic aspects of the wider narrative in this text. Imagination, this is pure imagination. The conclusion of this story is even more interesting than what you just heard. Our neighbours are imaginative people, listen! That man of Neishabur starts a rumour that Abu Muslim has not been killed and spreads it among the people. Listen to this!'

'I have to go, Katib! Didn't you hear the sound of the jeep's engine? This folder contains the dossier of those three prisoners. An appalling and tragic accident has taken place in the prison camp I'm commander of, and it's crying out for you to write a report about it, which will be much more interesting to read than the tales of our storytelling enemy!

Write your report on the basis of those documents if you like; if not, feel free to content yourself with the fabrications of our enemies. I am a soldier, Katib. When I put on this uniform, I swore an oath beneath the flag of our Arab homeland to remain steadfast to certain principles.'

'Coffee, Major? The coffee's ready! Two cups. Shall we drink together? Will you listen to me as I read the ending?'

'OK, read away and have done with it!'

'… he proclaimed vengeance for Abu Muslim's blood, the same Sunpadh, and let it be known that Abu Muslim had not been killed, [meaning that] when Mansur intended to kill him, Abu Muslim had chanted the great name of God and had turned into a white dove and flown out of his hands. And now he abides within an enclosure of copper, with his wives …'

'That was delicious. Great coffee. Better brewed than the first cup we had last night. Do you mean to say Abu Muslim turned into a dove in the hands of Caliph Mansur?'

'That was the very claim that Sunpadh of Neishabur used to assemble a group of followers who swore to follow in the steps of Abu Muslim …'

'Very well, Katib. In those days they … but let's not dwell on the question of the flag under which they fought us, my friend. My final word is to ask whether our katib is going to write a documented account or does he wish to turn into a white dove in the hands of Caliph Abu Mansur? Ultimately, that must be your decision, Abu Alaa! I sincerely hope and trust you won't turn into a dove! God be with you!'

'Farew – …'

# 10

I DIDN'T WANT TO HUMILIATE HIM, and I still don't. Our literature is filled with the humiliation of Arabs, all stemming from the frustration of defeat. So what was important to me in this situation was victory. I had to conquer, conquer the enemy's trench. I could kill him, right there in his trench. With a bullet, or my bayonet, or this wire loop hanging at my waist that was designed for strangling adversaries. But instead I handed it to that soldier to tie our captive's wrists together and then ordered him to remove his cartridge belt and tie it around his elbows, to pin them to his chest and back. He made me furious! But I couldn't just kill him in cold blood. The sun had just risen, but the small of his back was bathed in sweat. Sweat poured from his brow and ran down his neck. Evidently there was still some water left in his body, even though all the flasks in his trench were empty and his hip flask too. His eyes! His eyes tormented me. His gaze, that gaze ... it was with those eyes that he had spotted my five men before riddling them with bullets. If I were an executioner I would have plucked those eyes out of their sockets, only I lacked the callousness. It was thanks to my ability to turn into a dove that I had been able to descend the hill light-footed, crawl across the narrow valley between the two hills, and in ascending the far side turn into a serpent ... All I did was call him Saad ibn Abi Waqqas! And since I was certain he would never tell me his real name, from that moment onwards, Saad was what I would call him!

'Blindfold him, soldier! Tie a cloth over the prisoner's eyes. His crime is in those eyes and those fingers. Now make him walk down the hill and hold your white flag up, and if there are any flasks around take them and tie them together around your neck. I think I forgot to ask your name ... I did, didn't I? What did you say your name was?'

'Anoom,* sir!'

'Did you say Anoom?'

'Yes sir! I've taken his first-aid kit too ... with your permission.'

'Anoom?'

'Yes sir!'

'What's your unit?'

'Anoom, sir!'

'Which battalion?'

'The same, sir!'

'Regiment?'

'Same, sir!'

'Command centre?'

'I just mentioned it, sir!'

'Dispatched from?'

'Same, sir!'

'Surname?'

'Same as before!'

'City, province, region, village, place of birth, etc ...'

---

* In old Persian, *anaam* means 'human' – this is not a name and sounds nonsensical.

'Anoom, Captain sir!'

'I'm not a captain, boy! Were you captured alone?'

'No, Lieutenant sir! The other soldier was killed in the middle of the night. He'd gone mad from thirst.'

'Shouldn't you have been evacuated back behind enemy lines by now?'

'The enemy's reserve units were routed. He was confused. He'd lost his men and ... maybe he wanted to keep us hostage. What's going on down there, sir?'

'Doomsday!'

'I'm serious, sir. Why are we going down to the base of the valley? Wouldn't that be a fatal error? This Saad could shoot our boys so easily from up there. It's a trap down there. It's been three years and seven months since I joined the army. Down there it's a trap, sir!'

'Death and water. We won't stay long. Water, the water tank is down there. We'll take some water, see to our boys and then try to break out. I've positioned someone behind a machine gun up there too, if he survives until water arrives.'

'Did you say a water tank? Water? Water! Water! Where is the water? Where?'

'Under the brow of this very hill we're climbing down. You can't see it from this side.'

'You're right, sir!'

'Saad should walk two steps ahead of you. Pull the blindfold up from his eyes, just enough so he can see his feet. Otherwise he'll fall over, and dragging his carcass along will become our responsibility! We'd probably have to call a bone-binder for him as well! We'll make him wait at a distance of about five paces from the water and… When you've filled the first flask, pass it to me. Maybe our boys are still alive?'

'And after that, sir, then can I …'

'Why not? But don't forget we have two more men up there.'

'But if I don't drink some water soon, I won't have the strength to climb that hill.'

'You can do both at the same time. You're an agile young man, and experienced!'

'Yes, sir. Of course, sir!'

'This is a delegation. I will give water to the five, and you to those two.'

'Yes, one captive and one jamoo! I'll go, sir. Affirmative, sir!'

'Stick the white flag in the ground above the water tank … so it can be seen from all directions.'

'Of course, sir, it is done, sir!'

His upper body was naked from the waist up, and his skin was bruised all over. He weaved to left and right and ran and tumbled – literally tumbled down the hill to reach the bottom. The sound of flasks bumping along the ground and the rocks and the clods of earth immediately died away and a thin wisp of dust was all that remained of his trail; and the smell of water, the fragrance of water arose and I could feel it imprint itself on my olfactory sense – the scent of a drop of water that had fallen upon the earth. That soldier was a sight to behold, half-naked and entwined around the boulders; he clambered over them like a jungle cat. He returned, and tossed two full flasks into our trench, behind

Jamoo's machine gun, then twisted his body and with his back to the thorn-covered hill descended in my direction, having been ordered to gather our men's bodies and to lay them out in a line. He hadn't drunk any water himself yet. Or maybe he had. How else could he summon up such strength? I walked towards our boys, our comrades. The first one was dead. His hand was freezing cold. The second was dead, too. He must have been killed a bit later, as the vein on his neck was not yet completely cold. The third was still alive. I lowered the flask to his lips, but he refused it, and I realized after a brief moment of incomprehension that he was pointing at the fourth soldier. But the fourth man had surrendered his soul and so had the fifth. I returned to the third, knelt down next to him and brought the mouth of the flask to his lips, which were cracked and parched from thirst. With what little strength was left in his hand, he took the flask from me – very slowly, as if reaching for a faraway object – and tilted it, pouring the water onto the ground beside his head and neck. He muttered something; I lowered my head and brought my ear closer to hear his voice, and I heard him say: 'Are you satisfied? Are you satisfied with me? Are you satisfied with me now?' And his eyes remained open until I placed the palm of my hand over his eyelids and closed them. Now his eyes stayed closed. I put my hand on his still-warm brow and looked up at the sky. Oh God! My soldier was standing next to me, staring at the water glugging out of the flask. I motioned for him to pick it up. He picked up the flask and his gaze transferred to the stout captive who, unable to stand any longer, had slumped to the ground. I stood up.

The soldier looked at me and exclaimed: 'You're drenched in blood, Lieutenant!' I didn't wait for him to ask what we should do next. I told him to drink some water and to give some to our portly prisoner as well. He hated him. I did too, but what's to be done? Captives shouldn't be killed, right? He was the same person whose bullets failed to miss their target. He returned and gave the water flask to me; he wanted me to drink. 'You're groggy, sir, have a drink!'

'So you can see it too, soldier?'

'See what, sir?'

'These, all this, can't you see them? You can't? They're all around us. Can't you see? Shroud and flask. Look, look! You're thirsty, brother. Drink some water! Look, look! What a radiant day of resurrection! Helmets and boots and belts. One salutes the sun, one salutes water. One prays to the sky, one prays to the earth. One by one they emerge, from the shelter of the earth, from the fissures in the valley of death, from all around the vine-clad hills and passes both old and deep, shabby and antique, out of the ground, out of the graves, like the strange growth and blossoming of stones and thorns. Layer upon layer of earth cracks and blossoms into bodies. Shrouded figures, shroudless figures. Banners in hand or insignia on the tip of a spear. Their insignia is a frayed scrap of cloth, a tattered rag. Ragged black, ragged white, ragged purple, green, magenta and violet and red, multi-coloured. Colours discoloured. A body covered in tattered garments and carrying old weapons, withered and wretched, cold and frozen – the colour of the earth. As if fate has removed all primary colours from the ancient strata. Their boots have rotted and disintegrated, and many feet and hands lie there, naked and dismembered. Eyes are missing from their sockets. That one there has a robe draped around his body, while another sports crestless armour and a sash. It's impossible to tell which is friend or foe. Shredded garments and wounded feet, they emerge all together, all at once, propping themselves up on each other's shoulders, not caring who is a comrade or who is an enemy. Out they come, these men who have trodden arduous paths, hailing from the days of cuirass and stirrups and power and glory and will, their eyes empty. With armbands and ankle-bands, warriors' sashes and belts hung over their forearms, they keep on coming, sprouting from the earth, layer upon layer. Tired and parched, their ranks swelling and, thirsting after the scent of earth and water, they all begin streaming in the same direction. Though they do not recognize each other's insignia, they are familiar with each other's tongues, and perhaps with each other's souls, as well … But where is that voice coming from? It is not the voice of a single person, but of thousands from within the ancient ground of God. Where is that voice, in what place and from where? What is that voice and what am I?'

Bewilderment engulfed me, bewilderment and a sense of wonder that passed my understanding. I became confused as I looked, it baffled and confounded me … They kept on emerging from the strata of soil and stone and pebbles. They rose to the surface, every generation of mankind, one by one until they formed a vast multitude from the past. On and on they came, a leather rag clutched in a hand here, and a garment-clad half of a body there, some shroudless, some shrouded, but all gasping for breath, streaming in different directions, like a question without an answer, without looking at each other. Some bowed in salutation to the sun, others to the earth, some prayed to the sky, others to the water and stone. Where is my *qibla*?* Where is it? Where is my temple? My mosque? Where is my monastery, my temple, my synagogue and my fire? Where are my horse and my fire? My *qibla*, my sun and my temple … Where are my house and my nest? The river of souls merges and merges, then widens … wider and wider and wider …! One salutes the water, one salutes the sun and one salutes the earth!

'Can you hear that, soldier? Can you hear the voices?'

'Drink some water, sir! Please drink. You're hallucinating! You can barely stand upright! I'm holding you up. Your brow is drenched in cold sweat. If you give up, what shall I do? I know the first thing I'll do is kill the prisoner, that's for sure! So drink, drink some water, Lieutenant, sir! We're in the worst possible situation. Don't just take a gulp, drink some more!'

'I'm drinking, I'm drinking. But you can see it too, can't you, soldier?'

'What is it I'm supposed to see, sir?'

'You really can't see it, then?'

'What, sir? Please, I beg you, get a grip … you saw with

---

* The *qibla(h)* is the direction in which Muslims must face during prayers, defined by the position of the *Ka'aba*, the sacred cube-shaped structure within the Great Mosque at Mecca.

your own eyes what happened. We did our best. You poured water onto his lips and forehead yourself. I'm talking about the third soldier. But he chose to take the flask from your hand and empty it on the ground. Rest assured, by the time you got to him he'd already whispered his *ashhad** a thousand times. You heard for yourself how he departed this world asking for forgiveness and reconciliation. I've collected their identification tags. All five of them. I'll keep them separately. All five of them dead for the sake of getting some water ... As per your orders, I've laid all five of them in a row, facing the *qibla*. Now I'm waiting for your next command. It was you who said that it doesn't do to linger in the valley for too long. It just takes another madman to appear up there. Then we'll be finished, too. The rising sun only makes it even more dangerous to stay in this vile valley of doom!'

'So you honestly don't see anything? Not a thing?'

'Sure ... I can see that oaf there, our prisoner. He's our responsibility now, too. If only I could finish him off. He can't stand upright either, he fell down over there, and nearly passed out!'

'Didn't I order you to give him some water?'

'I did, though, sir. Otherwise he'd have gone to hell by now. Even so, he can't stand up, because he's so overweight!'

'Give him some more, then.'

'How much?'

---

*Refers to *tashahhud*, a portion of the prayer recited at the time of conversion to Islam. It is also chanted before martyrdom to ensure passage to heaven.

'Until he's had his fill! Until he explodes, for all I care!'

'May I ask, sir ...'

'Ask what?'

'If you're alright?'

'Couldn't be better! Say what you were going to say.'

'In such circumstances ... I mean, after suffering from thirst for such a long time, if a person drinks too much water, will he explode? Or die suddenly? I've certainly seen with my own eyes how men can pass away just like that!'

'A flask of water can hardly kill a man, can it?'

'No, sir. But ... we don't have much left either ...'

'It's not much, I know. The dying, the thirsty ... but we've been stuck here for too long. Just tell me what we should do with our men. I can't leave them on this scorching ground under the sun. What should we do with them, soldier? What was your name again?'

'Anoom, sir. I've commandeered a spade from the enemy trench, sir. Allow me to bury them right here, or on the flank of the hill. Close to the water tank. You know how to recite the death prayer, don't you?'

'First we must recite our intention. But I'd like us to take them with us. My heart won't let me abandon them here. In this narrow pass.'

'We could take them with us, sir, sure. But where to? I don't have a compass on me. If I'd had one I wouldn't have been captured. What about you, can you work out which direction we should go in?'

'I unravelled a ball of string behind us so we could retrace our steps, but heavy bombing has churned up the ground. So we'll just have to take them to our own trench for now. Now go and get that giant up on his feet, will you? We need him to help us carry his victims. Go and give him something from the flask!'

'Then what, sir?'

'I'll sling a body over my shoulder and climb the hill. You take another and the giant can carry a third. Just make sure you keep your eyes on him.'

'I'll lay one body across his neck and shoulders without untying his hands. And I'll tie his feet together so that he can't pull any tricks while he's carrying his burden. Like leg shackles! In just two round trips we can carry them all up to behind our machine gun. It'll be fine if you just take one body, sir! The two of us, Saad and I, will do the second round. You can go back down to fetch some more water. There aren't many intact flasks left, but … in the best case scenario the radio telephone might start working again. Then we could call for an ambulance, assuming one can cross the front line.'

'Cross an area that's in the enemy hands? Very well, remove his blindfold and take him over to the bodies. Let him see the results of his handiwork at close quarters!'

'His men were lying about all shot to bits too, sir, as a result of our firing … and our men just went down to that accursed water tank. One by one … I couldn't stop them. Thirst and the sight of the water tank had made them take leave of their senses, every last one of them! What could I do? They were young. They were volunteers who didn't really have any understanding of military discipline yet. Instead, they just took the idea of martyrdom for granted. Each person putting the others before himself …'

'So what preventative actions did you take that failed, Lieutenant?'

'Well, I tried talking reason and logic to them, telling each of them what his duty was. I stressed the need for order and discipline. But some of them had been through no more than six weeks of training. I tried every which way I could, sir, I even told them stories and parables! But it was useless, sir, impossible. They would have started fighting among themselves in the trench and I wanted to avoid that at all costs! After the heavy bombing and the annihilation of the reserve forces, when our line of communication was broken, the men's mindset changed completely. The radio telephone only transmitted a single message, saying that we couldn't expect relief any time soon. And that we should act on our own initiative. That made things worse than they were already. I was the group's senior officer. Commander of my unit. Before the destruction of the reserve forces the men had a certain look about them, but afterwards the atmosphere was quite different. That was only natural. I tried to pretend I wasn't afraid, but … it was a dead end, sir. We'd come to a dead end. Enemy forces had taken the ground behind us, and in front of us were lines of enemy troops who gunned down anything that moved. Hunger and then thirst grew. We were forced to stay in the trench for days on end. Our tactics switched from offensive to defensive and then from defensive to explosive, punctuated with moments of reckless hope. What would you have done in my place, sir?'

'That's not the issue here. You were the one in command, and you decided on a particular course of action!'

'It was inevitable, sir. Inevitable! As deranged as they were, my men knew that they didn't want to die of thirst in their own trench! Between staying put and dying or going to find water and saving the others they chose the second option. Hoping that they might succeed. Their action was the height of honour and self-sacrifice as well as of desperation and helplessness. Is it my fault that war knows nothing of honour? Each of them went down in the hope of rescuing the remaining men from certain death, even if the price was martyrdom. But that Saad who I took captive was extraordinarily skilful and every shot of his found its target!'

'Why didn't you kill him?'

'Sir?'

'I asked why you didn't kill him in the trench there and then, when you came upon him and put the tip of your bayonet on his spine and pressed the muzzle of your sidearm to his temple?'

'Yes … I couldn't, sir.'

'You couldn't? What do you mean you couldn't? Your bayonet was pointed right at his spine, wasn't it?'

'Yes sir. It would have been possible to shove the bayonet into his spine and he would either have died instantly or been crippled for life. I could also have blown out his brains with my pistol. But I couldn't. I can't kill a human being.'

'What? You can't kill a human being? Why did you go to war, then?'

'To do my duty and if necessary to kill soldiers.'

'I don't understand. You're not making any sense!'

'It's quite simple, sir. Soldiers are different from human

beings. You can't see a soldier's face from far away. They usually move in groups, as enemy units. You kill a nameless opponent. A soldier or soldiers are killed with your weapon and they fall to the ground. But a human being … No! That morning, the small of my prisoner's back was drenched in sweat, which left a trail of perspiration on that part of his jacket. The smell of his sweat reached my nostrils and I saw him shiver suddenly, as if emptied of life! His heart beat louder and louder as I stood over him. Louder by the minute. I could hear him breathing. Panting like a trapped bull. Straight away, he dropped his gun and one of our men – who he had taken prisoner – pulled the gun towards himself with his foot. He surrendered. He dropped his weapon and surrendered. Complete surrender. It felt like his wish had come true as he was taken prisoner. I saw him turn into someone different, into himself, into a person. The man was exhausted. The unit under my command was only responsible for scouting and reporting the situation at the enemy front line to the relevant command centre. We weren't a combat group. Although, naturally, we hadn't gone to the front just for fun!'

'Lieutenant … there is a note in this file to the effect that you volunteered for military service. You were an only child, which would have given you a reasonable excuse to stay in the reserves. But you insisted in no uncertain terms on going to war. Tell us in your own words … what subject did you study at university?'

'Pure maths, sir!'

'Pure maths? What's the use of pure maths?'

'It has all sorts of uses – and none!'

'How so?'

'Like pure poetry. Pure maths is like pure poetry. Like sheer poetry. It may or may not have a use. To be honest, I wanted to become Khwarizmi, but I turned into Ayn al-Quzat! I was thinking of studying astronomy but it never happened and I ... was *besmel*ed!'

'Lieutenant, could you tell us your main motive for volunteering to join the army?'

'The enemy's presence, the presence of the enemy, the homeland and a sense of duty and ...'

'Could you please describe your family circumstances to this court, fully and frankly? We are all soldiers here, regardless of our varying degrees of responsibility and rank. You had a sister, too, a medical student, didn't you? Isn't it true that she disappeared during the troubles?'

'No, sir. She turned into a dove as well!'

'A dove? What do you mean? Was her name "Dove", or are you speaking figuratively...?'

'No, sir, she became a dove. They took her away and for weeks there was no news of her. Sometime later, one morning when I was getting ready to go to college, as I put my foot up on the edge of the pool to tie my shoelaces, I noticed that Mahi had turned into a dove and was sitting on the roof: "Good morning, Koochik,"* she said. "I've become a dove! It was you who told me people can turn into doves!" As I stood there, gazing up at her, she asked me to burn her clothes if they were ever sent home. She told me they were dirty and unhygienic. She'd been a bit of

---

* Farsi, meaning 'little' or 'little one'.

a cleanliness freak since childhood, our Mahi, very obsessive-compulsive. That's why she was studying psychiatry. Then she flapped her wings and flew off and every morning thereafter I'd hear her voice from the rooftop. But I couldn't see her anymore. Yes, sir, Mahi became a dove too!'

'Then what happened?'

'Then … it didn't take more than six months for our mother to die of grief.'

'And after that?'

'Before he went mad, my father moved to another province to stay with the family of his sister, who had a daughter betrothed to me, called Mahsa.* We called her "Dove" too. She was studying architecture. But when they rescued her from the cellar of the ruined house she didn't have any fingernails left, from clawing at the cellar walls to try and find a way out. Three days had passed since the house was bombed.'

'Why? Why did that happen? Was she anti-revolutionary too?'

'No, sir. She studied interior architecture and usually did her homework in the cellar of the house, in the empty, shallow pool. In fact, that old cellar was her study. When one of the enemy missiles hit my aunt's home, Mahsa was preparing for her thesis exam in the cellar's empty pool with one of her university friends. After struggling for three nights and days to escape, they were weak and exhausted. And they were terrified too, sir. They found them lying side by side, with their heads on each other's

---

* A female name, meaning 'Moon-like'. Mahi is a nickname for Mahsa.

shoulders. Would you like to see Mahsa's photograph, sir? But no, I'd better not … it's a family photo. Her head isn't covered. I'll describe her to you instead. She's got auburn hair, hazel eyes and a pale complexion. It's a full-length portrait.'

'So after that you decided to join up and fight?'

'No, it was long before that, sir. Please don't belittle me! I was already at the western front when that incident took place. No one had the heart to tell me until I went on a five-day leave.'

'Did that incident have any effect on your mental state, Lieutenant?'

'It must have had some effect, I guess. The dovecotes at the house were flattened too.'

'Lieutenant! I want you to listen carefully to what I'm about to ask you and make sure that your answer is correct and precise!'

'I'm all ears, sir!'

'You … Mister Koochik-Kameh, nicknamed Kehtar,* you caused the martyrdom of five of our brothers while you yourself … How is it that you didn't feel any remorse and weren't afflicted by guilt after your subordinates were martyred while you … survived?'

'One, they were my brothers too. Two, I didn't achieve that honour because I was going to be *besmel*ed. Three, I am not the one who has stayed behind and is being inter-rogated now; my soul is a dove who will fly away into the

---

* Koochik-kameh and Kehtar respectively mean 'one who has little ambition' and 'lesser' in Farsi.

blue skies over our town after this formality. Four, my conscience is deeply wounded, and henceforth, until the end
of the world, every day a drop of blood will fall from the
throat of the dove that I am; a drop of blood will fall on
the clay roof of this house. Five, I am a *besmel*ed dove. Six,
don't send me to the lunatic asylum, please don't!'

'Lieutenant sir or Captain sir, or fellow soldier! Forgive
my asking, but we're mates now, right? Of course, you are
the commander in charge, but ... I'm curious since now and
then you speak to yourself ... for example, this "*besmel*",
you say this word more than any other, and along with that
sometimes I hear the word "dove" too ... dove ... before all
this I liked doves as well. But I didn't like pigeon-fanciers.
When I was a kid I heard one of them had sneaked up to
the rooftop of his rival at midnight, into the pigeon loft or
pen, and he decapitated all of his rival's pigeons! Because,
the day before that, one of his opponent's racing pigeons
had won the homing race. The races were run like this:
they'd each take one of their racing pigeons to an unfamiliar town, and the accompanying referee would count from
one to ten, and on ten the pair of pigeons were released
and flew off. The poor birds had to fly back to their home-
town and their nest from that unfamiliar town, covering
eighteen or twenty leagues in the process. On the roof-
tops expert impartial referees were waiting along with the
friends of the pigeon-fanciers, seated or standing, in the
shadows. As soon as they'd released the pigeons, the owners
and the referee would get back into the car and drive fast
so that they'd be back in time to see the birds return. If the
car didn't break down on the way, they'd arrive at the same

time as the pigeons. The competing pigeons were usually male, as they had a strong instinct to get back to the nest and the female birds. This time, as bad luck would have it, one of the pigeons still hadn't reached maturity and on reaching the town he became confused and returned to his roof and nest a few minutes later than his winning rival. In situations like that, a bit of skulduggery is quite normal, if you can get away with it. It is a rule that no one else's pigeons may fly on the afternoon of a race, but even so a crooked competitor may persuade one of his mates to fly his pigeons. So when the competing pigeons reach the town, if one of them isn't mature and experienced, it'll get caught up among the rogue pigeons and precious minutes will be lost before it realizes its mistake, detaches itself from the flock, and returns to its own loft. By which time the race will have been lost. The referees even count the seconds; anyway, that's precisely what happened on this occasion between the two rival pigeon-fanciers. I don't know exactly what the stake was in this instance … they could bet anything, money or something else … for instance, maybe the prize this time for the winner was his opponent's best bird, which the loser would have to surrender without demur, as well as paying travel expenses and the referees' fee. Of course, the defeated rival stood to lose a lot, but most importantly his honour and pride, since he'd no longer been seen as the town's top pigeon-fancier. So at midnight, the loser had gone up to his rival's rooftop, into the loft, and … decapitated all the poor birds!'

'What a dreadful crime … how ghastly!'

'I was very small when I heard about this. I didn't cry.

But I wanted to go with someone to the pigeon-fanciers'
hangout. I wanted to look into the eyes and faces of each
and every one of them and find out which wicked bastard
had had the heart to do such a horrible thing. But my
family wouldn't let me. They told me they were all cut-
throats to a man. That same evening, late at night, word
spread that the rivals had brawled and knifed each other,
cut each other open. There was a policeman in our neigh-
bourhood; his name was Nabi Sebil. He brought the news
from the police station. "See?" said my family on hearing
this, "We don't belong to that world." I see I've drifted away
from the matter in hand, Lieutenant sir, but ... they called
them pigeon-fanciers. As in, they loved pigeons. Then how
is it possible that someone who is in love with pigeons can
bring himself to decapitate about eighty or ninety pairs of
them in a couple of minutes?'

'Madness! Excessive love is a hair's breadth away from
madness. There have been lovers who have killed their
loved ones out of sheer love! Greed, greed and avarice are
vile motives that can sometimes lead – indeed, often have
led – to bigger crimes as well. Did you fill the flasks, all
of them? Okay. I'll take that spade, too. Give the giant
some more water, and call him Saad! He won't tell us his
real name. We don't need to know it, anyway. He'll tell us
everything when the time comes. I'll take the flasks, these
weapons, this spade and anything else that might be useful.
You carry one of the two remaining bodies and Waqqas
will carry the other one. There's nothing else left here.
Right, let's get moving!'

'Yes, sir! But just to satisfy my curiosity, please, I know

it's very forward of me to ask, but that's the first time I've ever heard that phrase, that word.'

'Which phrase?'

'*Besmel*!'

'Okay, up the hill we go. Saad first and you after him, but keep your distance and don't walk immediately behind him. We don't know if he's mad enough to suddenly turn on you, hurl himself and what he's carrying on you and set you all rolling down the hill. I'll walk backwards in front of him and point his own gun at him, so he knows I can send him to hell with no chance of missing. Still, you shouldn't walk directly behind him. Walk parallel to him! How long did it take you to get up the hill the previous time?'

'Less than fifty minutes when I was carrying a body. This time it might take about an hour. The first time, when I went up with no load, it only took me seventeen minutes to go up and come back down again. But from Saad's expression, I don't think he's capable of turning and moving nimbly. His hands are tied too. It'll be a miracle if he doesn't tumble down while he's climbing anyway. I'm ready … but …'

'I understand. Alright! Once we're up there, out of this valley of doom, there in the trench I will tell you all about *besmel*. We'll probably have to stay in the trench for the entire day and at nightfall find a way to break out, walk under cover of darkness and get ourselves to a friendly base. I'm not concerned on that score. Many's the night I've stared at the stars, and I know how to navigate by them, like the caravan leaders of old. We'll have all day in the trench for me to tell you the story of *besmel*, the story of becoming a dove, and the story of that lioness who has breasts filled with milk, who scours the desert for the lost ones who are dying of thirst and hunger. Immediately, without any delay or expectations, she feeds them her milk and shows them the way. Have you heard about that lioness? No! But … if we don't manage to get out of this valley of hell, or if dark clouds come and cover the sky and the stars are no longer visible, and if clouds of fire rain down upon us, then we'll see with our own eyes the meaning of the word you are seeking to understand. Right then, lift the body up onto his shoulders and fasten his legs to his neck with the cartridge belt. That way this Saad will know he'll be in even more trouble if he tries to shed his load and do a runner. Anything else to report?'

'Same as before, two or three petrol tankers parked beyond that bend in the road and no doubt there are other booby-traps concealed or buried all over the place! We didn't have time to investigate thoroughly. This pass is known as the Pass of Hell and it's been in enemy hands for months. Perhaps they've planted gunpowder in every grain of dirt. How can we tell?'

'Let's go, then … You know, I really wish you hadn't told me that story about those pigeon-fanciers … it was horrible. Ready, soldier?'

'Yes, sir!'

# 11

'THIS IS BAD! Very bad indeed, Major. You've entered my head, got inside my mind and created the most dreadful confusion. I was on the verge of finishing my work. The scene was there, right in front of my eyes. Everything was crystal clear. I could picture my characters, and understand their every motive. In my mind, I'd rehearsed everything that needed to happen. A small symbolic truce, avoiding the humiliation of either side, starting with a white shirt tied to a stick. It was simple, very simple. The two prisoners would leave the trenches holding white flags. They would descend the hill from either side, followed by the soldiers and their commanders, unarmed, and they'd all walk towards the water tank. They were all thirsty, they would drink water, greet each other and converse. They would wash the dust off their foreheads and sit for a little while in each other's company. They would see each other with their own eyes, not through the distorting lens of war, and they would realize that they felt no particular hostility towards each other. In that frame of mind, they would all be their real selves. They wouldn't be soldiers anymore. You've disrupted a small truce, Major, a symbolic peace. Isn't it the case that every war ends in peace? I was going to make this happen sooner. But you, Major, have entered my mind, penetrated my consciousness and thrown my thought process into disarray. You've thwarted my creativity! Why won't you let a person at least live in his own mind according to his own will!'

'You shouldn't have returned to your homeland, Abu Alaa, I do wish you hadn't. They wouldn't accept the suggestion I made with regard to you. I pleaded for leniency, in view of the friendship that has grown up between us during the time we've spent together. But they didn't approve of the idea. I tried to impress upon them that you needed rest. Rest in an asylum. If they'd seen things my way, you could have escaped with your life. You could have stayed there for some time and you'd have had plenty of time to reflect on your profession and your life. At the same time, it would have been an excuse for you not to write this report, which we now have to deal with. Or conversely, you could have made up your mind to write it after all, and then you would have been reprieved, and that would have been the end of it! But now … it's a different story. I have a message for you from the palace of the caliph Abu Ja'far: a short and clear message. Plus a gift – a pen, and a sidearm as well! A dossier, a copy of the dossiers of those three prisoners is still waiting on your writing desk. The message is very short, clear and concise. Either you write the report about those three prisoners or you will become a dove, by your own hand! I don't have permission to stay here any longer, Katib, and I'm not allowed to chat or discuss this with you either. The message is clear and all my attempts to convince them that you're suffering a nervous breakdown and need to be admitted to a mental hospital for a spell have fallen on deaf ears. I wish you good health, good mental and physical health. God keep you, Abu Alaa!'

'God keep you too, sir. God keep you! … But I can't even hold a pen with these weary fingers and withered wrist, Major, let alone a gun!'

'So just keep hold of it for self-defence!'

'I can't do it. I've never done military service. And even if I could hold a weapon, I wouldn't anyhow. How could I shoot another person? Even in self-defence! I just can't conceive of such an act!'

'Well, that's all we can do for you! You might find it comes in useful. Once again, may God keep you!'

# 12

EVERYTHING IS CLEAR until clouds suddenly blot out the sky. Surely not in this season? Dark, roaring clouds, growling. Under a duvet of dark grey and black clouds, Jamoo turns on his side and spontaneously presses the palms of his hands to his ears, as if he is unaware that he has rolled over and is not lying on his front anymore, but on his back, looking at the sky from the base of his machine gun. Not looking ... rather staring at the low ceiling of the sky. No, not staring, but drowning in the rumbling duvet of the sky. A sky that growls and roars in whichever direction you turn. Sometimes the roaring is fleeting and sporadic, while at other times it seems to reverberate all around; worse still, it has no specific origin. From all the points of the compass, these sounds, the roaring and the explosions, course and flow. The last time he had the lieutenant, the soldier and the captured man in sight, they were ascending the slope of the hill with tired and heavy footsteps. But then the sky had suddenly exploded and instantly turned black. Now he realized it was clouds of smoke that had sullied what had been a clear sky. From the lowest possible altitude at which aircraft could fly, a huge plume of smoke had billowed up, which grew so dense so quickly that it seemed as though it might darken and befoul the whole world. They were military aircraft, no question. Aircraft that were capable of bringing down a black rain, and that's exactly what they were doing. They rained down an infernal shower upon the entire valley of hell, setting off explosions. One after the other, a series of explosions, intermittent, near and far! What was it that was buried in the heart and shoulders of that valley of hell from whose depths smoke and black flames now belched, rising up to touch the remainder of the tattered duvet spread across the low dome of the sky? Up they billowed, obscuring the rocks on the flanks of the slopes, blackening everything as they went; and as they licked up, it seemed as though the tongues of fire were turning the hillsides into a furnace, whose intense heat could be felt as it reflected down upon the heart of the earth and on the stones and the trench, that same hand-dug ditch in which Jamoo had by chance ended up. And now that he had recovered his power of speech, he was screaming. With each scream, his mouth filled with acrid smoke, but he kept on screaming anyway, not knowing whether he was alive or dead. He didn't have a clue what had happened all of a sudden, and what was happening now. Round and round and round his head and his eyes swivelled ... as if the world were spinning around the head of this young man who had fallen into the depths of that ditch and who knew nothing, who could only scream; and the only way he could stifle his screaming was by grinding his face into the dirt and yelling into the earth ... until all his breath was exhausted and all he could do was wait for time to pass, for the earth to spin round, and for this unknown something, which was unlike anything he had ever known, to come to an end. Maybe it will resound in the ears and heart of the earth, that blood and ash-drenched scream of a teenager who from the bottom of his being yelled his anguish into the ground: Oh Gooodddd …

Yes … somewhere, at some spot here on planet Earth, a shell is propelled out of the muzzle of a heavy weapon. A leaden shell, heavy and destructive. We don't know the exact circumstances, and perhaps the person who orders a firing button to be pressed doesn't know either. Maybe a switch is flicked up or down instead. How can we know? All we are interested in is what happened afterwards and who was responsible for causing these clouds of smoke and fire to rise up above a pass, a ravine, a chasm – in any event, a target that did not appear to be an ammunition dump. What was this disaster that was unfolding before the eyes of a young man who had forgotten his own name, and his birthplace as well – who had just a random name, a meaningless word on his tongue, but who otherwise was completely mute, or rather dumb? Dumb and afflicted with instant loss of memory. Now his body felt racked with fatigue and aches, and his eyelids were heavy, weighed down by a thick layer of something whose colour he did not recognize, but which he imagined must be that of tar or – less dark – of smoke. He had been hurled into the depths of the trench, and each explosion had reverberated against an earthen wall whose surface was studded with stones and pebbles. He understands nothing now except that the world has been engulfed in such a ghastly silence that when he reflects upon it for a while, it appears to him more dreadful than the hell that went before. How much time had elapsed since it happened? Thousands of years or just a fleeting moment?

He lifted his head with difficulty, and with his handkerchief, now as black as tar, tried to wipe the thick layer of dirt off his eyelids; eventually he succeeded to the extent that he was able to open his eyes and look at the sky. Yes … it was completely blue – but strange! For no noise was coming from it. Beforehand he could hear the noise of the air, before this, some sounds could be picked up, the sound of the breeze or even the sound of silence, but now there was no sound at all. He tried to stand up. Bracing himself against the wall with his hands, he straightened his body. Once upright, he gazed around. There was silence and nothing else. He put his foot on the step of the trench, and the sun came into view, the wide dome of the sky and the earth. He climbed out. Not a single soul was visible, nothing! He walked towards the top of the hill. They were missing, the bodies were missing. He looked into the chasm. It was black like the belly of a furnace, silent and dark, and there was no sign of anyone or anything. The machine gun whose tripod he himself had secured in the ground was gone too. Everything had vanished! He looked at the sun. It had passed its peak and was declining towards sunset. He remembered that the fangs of the sun had sprouted when the lieutenant and the other two had climbed up and laid the bodies on a piece of ground and swiftly gone back down again. Yes, earlier on he had been able to make out someone's arms and shoulders, naked and bruised, and recalled that he had chucked two flasks full of water behind the machine gun, shouting: 'Catch!' Yes … he had heard a voice. He had heard the sound of a command from his own superior. He remembered that he had picked up the flasks, drunk half the water from one of them, and given the remainder to that handcuffed young man … a prisoner? But … where was he now? Before this all happened, he recalled that the prisoner had been lying on his front behind a pile of earth next to the trench. He walked over to where he had been lying, but there was no sign of him! The flask was gone too. What had happened? He climbed back down into the trench; the radio telephone was buried. Why was he bothering to dig it out? It wasn't working anyhow. Or maybe it was working and he couldn't hear anything! He tried to operate it. He couldn't hear the sound of his fingers working. He picked up the receiver and pressed it to his ear. Not a sound! When he replaced the receiver he saw it was soaked with blood … what had happened? What had happened to the head that remained attached to his body? … Fear gripped him. He put his hand on the trench step and stood stock still. Petrified. A dove? Yes … there stood a dove on the lip of the trench, perched on a clod of earth, looking at him and shifting around on its feet in a semi-circular motion. A second appeared, and then a third and a fourth, then a fifth – and in the same order they flapped their wings and soared upwards. And what about those drops of blood? How to explain them? In that darkness the doves were hard to see, but gradually more doves joined them, and forming a circle they flew, up and up against the background of a blue sky that stretched far, far away to the sea, that ancient gulf; the same place where the sea and the sky became one. All one single, smooth surface, the colour of Neishabur turquoise.

He couldn't hear the sound of the flapping of the doves' wings, that inexperienced young man, who, in thrall to his mind's imaginings, found himself enraptured by the sky and the soaring flight of the doves. The entire sky, which earlier that same morning had been obscured by rumbling black clouds and the infernal rain, was now decked out with the white of their wings. The lieutenant sir had told Jamoo another story, too. The story of the lioness who roamed the desert with milk-filled breasts. 'A lioness who does not discriminate between friend and foe, who seeks out the thirsty and the thirsty seek her.' So Jamoo must start moving, and begin to descend the hill, which was now draped in indigo as if in mourning for itself. It was during his descent that the shell-shocked young man caught sight of his prisoner at the bottom of a ditch, in a hole with his hands still tied behind his back. He didn't look in any better shape than Jamoo. For an instant, the prejudice of youth made him consider killing the captive. He did not have a firearm, just a knife as a defensive weapon. He drew the knife and approached the enemy solider. Killing him would not be difficult. His hands were tied behind his back and his feet were lashed together at the ankles, and the explosion had blown him from his original location, bowled him down the slope of the hill until he had fallen into a ditch, thus saving his remaining half-a-life. Knife in hand, Jamoo stood on the rim of the crater in front of the man and commanded him harshly to get up and walk! But the man in the hole could not get his body to move. All he managed was to half-open his eyes, just enough to cast a glance at his would-be killer; half a glance ... and then his eyelids closed again, as though he had no desire to look at anyone or anything. His posture in the ditch caused his head to tilt to one side, exposing his neck and making it seem as though he yearned for a hand holding a blade to cut the arteries and veins in his throat and end his life. It wouldn't make any difference; there was hardly any life left in him, anyway. So he did not react when he was suddenly confronted by a sinister and bloodied figure with a blackened face and bloodshot eyes, holding an unsheathed knife and standing close to his shoulder. He pictured the figure planting a foot on his chest, leaning over, grasping his hair with his claw-like hands, holding his head up and in a sawing motion severing his head from his body, leaving him for the vultures and hyenas that were so common hereabouts. But killing another person requires special circumstances and a special disposition. Maybe if the young man standing at the edge of the crater had had a firearm, his task would have been easier. A firearm and some distance were what was required. An instantaneous act. And even in those circumstances, the enemy shouldn't be lying prone and lifeless on the ground, or at least not be so close to death. The standing young man chewed his lips, unable to determine what taste it was that was leaching from his lower lip and pervading his tongue and taste buds. Fuel oil, gunpowder, metal, ash, dirt or a mixture of all those combined with the taste of blood and burnt human bodies? The hand clutching the hilt of the dagger was still trembling, as were his lips. He looked at the sky, but not a single dove was visible, even in the far distance. It felt as though he was saying 'Oh God!' as he stamped his foot on the ground, but he couldn't hear his own voice. Raising his voice, perhaps, he shouted: 'Oh God! What should I do? What must I do?' Again, he could not hear his own voice. He pressed his hands to his ears and bellowed the same words, with exactly the same result. He took his hands away and looked at his palms. His hands were partially covered with lumps of black and clotted blood ... he screamed and screamed and screamed, and in the silence of his screaming he did not realize he was running in the desert, until ... again he was standing by the head of that young man, his captive, whose life, in all probability, was slowly ebbing away from him. He stamped his feet on the ground to make the prisoner listen to him: can you hear my voice? I know you're in a bad way, but tell me that you can hear my voice. Well, can you? You ... sound ... voice ... hear? Or has my voice flown up to the sky with those doves? Blood ... check that no blood is dripping from my throat ... Or from my ears? Open your eyes. He told me that some doves, when they come to roost on the roof of their home loft, shed a drop of blood from their throat. That calms them, apparently, so that they can then fly on right through the night until daybreak. I haven't been *besmel*ed to become like that. Get up and talk to me! In whatever language you know. Just talk! I want to hear your voice. And tell me that you can hear mine! Can't you? Get up, otherwise what's to become of us in this endless desert? Look, I'll cut the strap binding your legs, there! Now you can get up. You didn't have any less water than me and your fate isn't any more dreadful than mine. I'm being tested, but you ... you wretched man ... maybe you didn't get to see your companions slain in front of your eyes, but I did. I saw each and every one of them perish before my eyes and now that I've gone insane you needn't fear me anymore! It's passed now, the moment I thought about killing you like a dog! I won't kill you, but you must stand up. We're the same, the two of us, like an apple cut in two halves. Now climb out of your grave and tell me if you can hear my voice. You can, can't you? Bring your ear close to my mouth, I am going to scream. What the hell is your name anyway? Zayd! I will scream your name, if you can hear it nod your head, like this. If you didn't hear me, shake it. Now I'm screaming: 'Zayd! Zayd! Zayd! Zayd!' No? You didn't hear me? My voice, you didn't hear my voice? No? Oh God … God … God … you said yourself that Khezr the prophet helps the lost and the miserable in the desert. So, O Khezr, hear my prayer! But if my voice is gone, how can it reach Khezr's ears? O prophet Khezr, you understand my intention, not for my own sake, but for the sake of this captive … make him talk! Zayd … now it's your turn to speak, say something, shout it! Here's my ear. Go on, shout into my ear! Shout louder, louder! Tell me something … please say something! You shouldn't have gone mute, and I shouldn't … shouldn't be deaf and dumb! It's not fair! All the time that honourable man was speaking to me and trying to encourage me, I was dumb, couldn't utter a single word. And now that my speech has returned to me – or at least I think it has – I can't hear any voices. Or any sounds. I couldn't hear his voice either. No doubt, he came to say farewell to me and said: 'Look, do you see now with your own eyes what I told you weren't just stories!' From within the maelstrom of darkness and explosions and fuel oil and gasoline and gunpowder that blackened the world, a white dove emerged, followed by other doves, with their brilliant white wings. Yes … he came, he spoke and I didn't hear him, because I can't. So move along there, Zayd! Don't make me mad! From the moment this dagger was entrusted to me, it hasn't cut anyone's throat. Don't make me cut you down because you're trying to escape. The smell of your blood will attract vultures; first of all they'll dig out your eyes and then, while you're still alive, they'll tear you limb from limb. Now I've said my piece. Whether you can hear me or not, that's not my problem. I've declared my intention; my actions from here on in are out of my control. Move on, we'll walk eastwards with our backs to the sunset. Either we will be killed on the journey, or we will encounter the lioness – either way, we'll find her or she'll find us. If she finds us she will show us the way. Just remember, I haven't done you any harm. First, I unshackled your hand from mine, leaving you to your own devices. Second, I untied your legs so you could walk. Earlier on, I shared a flask of water with you. And now we're in the same predicament, because there's no knowing whether we'll run into your forces or arrive at my base first; that puts us on an equal footing. But for the time being you're still my prisoner, not vice versa. In time, if we survive, I might yet decide to untie your wrists as well. If there is even an ounce of brain left in our heads, we will realize that my killing you will leave me alone in this desert, and the same applies if you were to kill me. When you've come to this conclusion too and I have accepted that you have, then

I will untie your hands. Did you understand my words? How can you, though, when you can't hear them? Oh God … please don't inflict me with madness! My blood is still hot! I might as well go mad on my own if I come to believe Lieutenant Kehtar does not exist anymore, that he will never return to his previous form. I will entrust myself to you for fear of madness, O God! May my voice be heard, or at least let me hear myself … let me know for sure that I no longer have any voice at all and that all these words are just thoughts – pure imagination. Let me know that I will be taken to that lioness who feeds milk to all who are thirsty, and who shows lost people the way. Amen!

# 13

THERE WERE MANY who were lost in the desert. Once lost, very few managed to escape the wasteland alive. And of those who survived, fewer still were able to explain why a person cannot walk in a straight line in the desert without a guide, without four-legged desert animals who know the way. Travelling at night in the desert is preferable for several reasons, the first being the possibility of navigating by the stars, exploiting the expertise and wisdom of the seasoned caravan leader and the leading camel. The second reason is the coolness of the desert air at night. It's as cool and breezy at night as it is hot and unbearable during the day. So if a couple of young men – immature and inexperienced, thirsty and desperate to reach safety – should take it upon themselves to travel in the daytime without any equipment, in particular the miraculous dial of a compass, they'd have not the slightest inkling why they were failing to make any progress. A certain amount of time must pass before they collapse, totally exhausted, and suddenly realize that they have been going round and round in a very tight circle. This will only become apparent when others chance upon their trail. How can this be? Well, it's because human legs and torsos are rarely straight and of exactly equal length. It's impossible for a person's legs to walk precisely symmetrically; everything depends upon the height, size, movement and joints of the individual's body. The same goes for the hands and shoulders and waist, and the neck and head and eyes as well; they're not at all as identical as they might appear at first glance. And that's why one keeps going round and round in the desert. The legs go round, the eyes go round. It's a constant turning that mirrors the mirage within your head and mind. Fatigue, thirst, helplessness and impending death – all these only multiply the likelihood of errors.

And so it was that the two young men walked round and round in circles, leaving the tell-tale trail behind them as they went. And on their circular trajectory, which would never arrive at any destination, they made every error possible. Dizziness and thirst, dumbness and muteness, illusions, mirage, fatigue and thirst all played their part. Each time they sat down to rest, they cast off what they thought were unnecessary encumbrances, totally discarding them, even their boots. Thick cotton socks may or may not have been able to save the soles of their feet from the heat of rocks and pebbles. But carrying one's boots is surely more arduous than tolerating the burning heat of the desert floor. Ultimately, all they had on was a single shirt, underwear and socks. Maybe they draped their uniforms over their heads to prevent the rays of light from penetrating the tiny pores in their skin, lest sudden and pure madness descend … and as they went round and round, with each turn the grip of exhaustion upon them became tighter and tighter until, during the final turn, much to their amazement, the soles of their feet suddenly felt wet. This is when they dropped on their bellies on a narrow strip where the ground was damp. Each grabbed a fistful of mud and squeezed it onto his tongue. Alas, the drops of moisture that fell upon their tongues tasted oily, but they weren't oil or petroleum. Even so, they felt compelled to stand up and follow the line of seemingly oily dampness. They pursued this path, on and on, until just before the sun went down. Sunset duly came and the mirage took on other forms. Whatever it was, it wasn't far off, yet it still was not close enough to be in sight. By this stage, their eyesight was growing very dim. Finally... a ghostly image, possibly a mirage, came faintly into view. But it turned out to be no illusion. It really did exist. A black slab of stone – heavenly in appearance – and a lioness sitting on top of it, propped against a pile of belts, boots, articles of clothing, cartridge belts, ancient-looking weapons, helmets covered in dirt and flasks mangled into each other, missile nose-cones and empty shell casings and broken radio sets, piles of old skulls among terracotta pots and pans, and shards of old spearheads now rusty and twisted, a few ancient helmets and mangled breastplates – perhaps from an old warrior's armour?

They approached the stone slab and stood in front of the supine lioness, who looked at them, the teats of her swollen breasts dripping with milk. She said – without speaking – what are you waiting for? For them to explode? For these breasts to explode? The pain of swollen breasts is no trivial matter. Either milk them or drink straight from them. Drink or milk them, my sons, I am that same mother lioness. Come closer to me and kneel before they explode, these breasts, and their milk is turned into blood. Come and drink, my sons. You are like my own twin cubs, who in just twelve days have aged twenty years. Drink, drink, drink, my children. Drink before the clouds rise once more to roar and rain black fire from the sky! But …

'They're rising. They're rising again!'